# WHEN WE MEET AGAIN

AVA GRAY

# ALSO BY AVA GRAY

# CONTEMPORARY ROMANCE

**Alpha Billionaire Series**

Secret Baby with Brother's Best Friend

Just Pretending

Loving The One I Should Hate

Billionaire and the Barista

Coming Home

Doctor Daddy

Baby Surprise

A Fake Fiancée for Christmas

Hot Mess

Love to Hate You - The Beckett Billionaires

Just Another Chance - The Beckett Billionaires

Valentine's Day Proposal

The Wrong Choice - Difficult Choices

The Right Choice - Difficult Choices

SEALed by a Kiss

The Boss's Unexpected Surprise

Twins for the Playboy

**Playing with Trouble Series:**

Chasing What's Mine

Claiming What's Mine

Protecting What's Mine

Saving What's Mine

**The Beckett Billionaires Series:**

Love to Hate You

Just Another Chance

**Standalone's:**

Ruthless Love

The Best Friend Affair

. . .

## PARANORMAL ROMANCE

### Maple Lake Shifters Series:

Omega Vanished

Omega Exiled

Omega Coveted

Omega Bonded

### Everton Falls Mated Love Series:

The Alpha's Mate

The Wolf's Wild Mate

Saving His Mate

Fighting For His Mate

### Dragons of Las Vegas Series:

Thin Ice

Silver Lining

A Spark in the Dark

Fire & Ice

Dragons of Las Vegas Boxed Set (The Complete Series)

### Standalone's:

Fiery Kiss

AVA GRAY

Wild Fate

# BLURB

**The man I've been in love with for the last six years doesn't even remember who I am...**

I've hidden some big secrets from Alexander Stone – my fake ex-husband.

Yes, we got married so he could secure his position as the CEO of his dad's company.

And I desperately needed the money he paid me.

The last six years have changed a lot of things, except for one.

I still remember the way he made my breath quicken when he came close.

His world would flip upside down if he finds out that I'm a mom.

A mom to *his* child.

It's a secret that I would do anything to protect.

The guilt of keeping that from him worsens every time he touches me.

But what happens when he realizes that I'm the same woman he once married?

And that I have another secret that would change the course of his life forever.

# 1

## ABIGAIL-SAM

"You're going to have to stop moping around after that asshole," Michelle announced after she took one look at me.

I was slumped over the counter, barely propping my head up on my limp wrists. Gravity felt stronger as the afternoon dragged on.

"You are scaring customers away."

"I'm sorry," I managed before another cascade of tears fell from my eyes.

"Oh honey, you are really hurting, aren't you?" Michelle came to the back of the counter and wrapped her soft, strong, arms around me. She provided comfort and solace when I didn't have anyone else who cared a thing about me.

I pressed my face into the crook of her neck and clutched her arms as I bawled with the pain of a thousand years. She stroked my hair and made other comforting sounds before she began ordering the rest of her crew around.

"Josh, don't worry about those dishes, I need you running the front counter."

"But…"

I could hear the conversation around me. It didn't mean I could stop sobbing or could pay much attention to it. Michelle held me for a really long time. At one point I think she was even talking to a customer when she said something about sometimes you just need a mom's hug. I didn't have a mom, at least not anymore. Michelle was now my mom. She said she adopted me when I started to work for her, and she learned my story.

Actual mom or not, her hugs were the best. Even when my heart was shattering and being ground to dust, I needed her support. Any other boss would have told me to get my shit together and go back to work. Or they would have put me in the kitchen to wash dishes so no one could see me. I didn't even want to think about the possibility of being fired over this. That of course, would just be the icing on the cake of my week.

Gradually, Michelle got me to move into the back. Niagara Falls continued to gush from my eye holes. That's all they were to me at this point, holes where my eyes should have been. I couldn't see, I was crying too much.

She brought me a glass of water. I struggled to sip it around my gulps for air.

"I'm sorry," I finally managed to say.

"Grief sometimes hits you unexpectedly like that. It happens."

"Grief?"

"Heartbreak is grief. It's a massive loss. Your body reacts the same way as if someone you loved died. We've all been through it. But it still doesn't make it any easier to know everyone has felt this pain, isn't it."

I shook my head. It didn't make the ache in my chest and the pounding in my head any better.

"You think you can handle washing dishes for the rest of the day?"

I nodded. "Michelle." My voice quavered; I was too nervous to ask. "Can I have the morning off? I have to find someone to help me move and get everything out of the apartment by ten on Friday."

"Do you have to move out so soon? Surely, you can take until the end of the month?"

I shook my head. My brain felt like it was sloshing around in a sea of tears. I was lightheaded, and a bit dizzy.

"Shit, Abigail-Sam, when was the last time you had something to eat? You are as pale as a sheet."

She got up and bustled out into the shop before returning with a doughnut held in a paper wrapper.

"Eat this," she said as she shoved the pastry at me.

I took a bite. I sighed and felt the tension in my shoulders ease up a bit. We sold the best doughnuts. A Mexican bakery from the other side of town delivered them every morning. They were so good, soft and sweet. Eating one was like eating a sugar cloud. I hummed in my short moment of contentment.

"Now tell me what's going on," she demanded.

I wiped the side of my mouth before I started talking. "David hasn't been paying rent."

"Shit."

"The landlord served me the last notification papers yesterday. They said I had forty-eight hours to vacate before I would be thrown out. I had a full-blown melt down on the guy. Crying, panicking. I even threw up. I asked him what was going on, and he told me that last month's rent hadn't been paid, and this month's hadn't either."

I took another bite of the doughnut as fortification to get through this story.

"He said he had given David the late rent notice and that David just laughed at him."

"So, David knew this was going to happen to you?"

I nodded. "He definitely set me up. He couldn't just break up with me and shatter my dreams. No, he had to destroy me. The lease is in my name. So, it's my rental history that's damaged, my name is even on the electricity bill. I expect that to get shut off any second now. So, with no electricity, and rent default, it all stacks up as justification to evict me. Anyway, I explained everything, and the landlord gave me a twenty-four-hour extension."

"How much stuff do you need to move out? Where are you going?"

I let out a defeated sigh. "I was too upset last night to even begin to think about what I needed to do. I got as far as stuffing clothes and bedding into my luggage. I need to get moving boxes, I need to find someone to help, and I need to find a storage unit."

Michelle nodded. "Okay, let's work on a little plan, do some brainstorming. Do you think you can stay for an hour or two more, and we can work and talk?"

I nodded. She was such a good person to me. And helping me think through all of this. I shoved the rest of the doughnut in my mouth and gulped down the remainder of the water.

Michelle patted me on the shoulder. "Go rinse your face and neck with cool water. It will help you feel better."

With a clean face and puffy eyes, I started to collect the bus buckets from the front of the cafe. I dumped everything in the sink and began the pre-wash routine. Rinse all visible food particles off, then shove it all into the dishwasher. Bathe in the steam as the dishwasher chugged along. Open, let everything sit until it was no longer hot enough to melt the flesh from my hands, unload, restock, and do it all over again.

It was a physically demanding job, the lugging of dishware back and forth. Sure, a single plate isn't that heavy, but a stack of twenty can be.

"Okay, you have two days to get out of your apartment," Michelle started.

She had pulled out some paperwork and set up on the closest prep table instead of sitting in her office. She did her paperwork task, and I did the dishes.

"How much furniture are we talking about?" she asked.

"I don't know. I don't know what will be there when I get home this evening. David has slowly been moving his stuff out. Last week it was his X-box and clothes. When I got home yesterday the kitchen table and chairs were gone."

"He's taking your furniture?"

"Yeah," I hated admitting that he was cleaning me out. He had taken the X-box and the TV. "I figure the more he takes, the less I have to move."

Michelle chuckled. "That's a good outlook. I can't believe he hadn't been paying rent."

"Me either." It still felt like a punch in the gut to think about how the landlord had sneered and spit at me, like I was nothing more than trash. And here I was telling Michelle the same thing. "It was finally David's turn to pay rent. He was so proud of himself too. Like he was Mr. Big. I feel like such an idiot. We agreed he could have his first paycheck to play with. I should have insisted he give me half for rent or something. But no, I agreed. He worked hard to graduate; he deserved some reward."

"You're the one who deserved the reward, Abigail-Sam. You have worked hard to put that boy through college. You paid his rent; you kept him fed. Did he at least buy you something with his play money?"

I turned around and pulled my sleeve up a little higher. Right above my left elbow was a little tattoo of a bird.

"Oh, you got a dead pigeon tattoo."

I could tell from the tone of Michelle's voice she thought it was crap. And it was. David wanted to surprise me, and I had trusted him, and his choice of art. And now I had a tattoo of a dead bird on my arm.

"Would you still be going to school when the semester starts?"

"I don't know how. I have to find a place to live and come up with a deposit. With this eviction on my credit history, that means I'll have to foot an even bigger deposit, if I can even find a place."

I slammed the rack of dirty dishes into the washer and closed the cover with a heavy thunk. I rested my forehead against the warm machine and then began rhythmically pounding against it.

"It was supposed to be my turn. David was going to take care of me. He was going to pay the rent and pay the bills so I could go to school and focus on homework."

"I know, I know. He's turned out to be a real jerk for doing this," Michelle said.

"What you need is a sugar daddy. Someone older who wants you to be happy and is willing to pay for all your needs."

I turned to look up at Josh. He gave me a stupid grin.

"Are you going to be my sugar daddy?" I asked.

He shook his head. "I'm too young, and too poor. I'm in the market for a sugar mama myself."

# 2

## ALEX

Staring out the window of what should have been my office, I didn't focus on the city. It sprawled beyond the view and was quite the sight. Right now, I was more interested in the reflection of what was happening behind me.

It felt like everything had been going on behind my back for years, why change now?

This had been my father's office, and when he passed rather suddenly five years ago, it should have become mine. That's not what happened.

Under the guise of giving me time to be ready, my uncle Roy and my mother staged a bit of a business coup. My own mother worked with my father's brother against his own son. I had been raised to run this company when my father retired. Only he had been reluctant to hand over the reins.

He should have retired a good ten years earlier, but no, he wanted to maintain control, and in the end, he died, never having time to enjoy all that wealth he had accumulated.

I enjoyed my wealth, and for some reason that enjoyment was some kind of proof that I wasn't fiscally mature enough to run a company. They treated me like some kind of toddler. I was very aware of where my money came from, I wasn't about to piss that away.

I liked my toys too much to do anything to get in the way of my continued ability to afford and maintain them. Apparently, my mother seemed to think that my latest acquisition, a Ferrari 296 GTB, was proof positive I simply wasn't ready.

"And what would have been a responsible car Mother? A minivan?"

I turned around to face them. They looked shocked that I was paying attention.

"A family vehicle could be seen as you being ready to take on some responsibility," my uncle declared.

"A minivan would be a good start. A steady girlfriend would be a better start."

I let out a sharp bitter laugh. "No woman is going to want to go out with me if I show up for a date in a minivan."

"That is not the right kind of woman you should be dating. You want one who is ready for a family. You are thirty-six Alexander, when are you going to make me a grandmother?"

"The only people who drive minivans are teenagers, or people who already have a family. You want me to make you a grandmother? That's more likely going to happen if I show up in a Ferrari."

They stared at me, as if they truly thought I wasn't getting it. I didn't want to be crude in front of my mother, but I felt like they were pressuring me.

"I never would have married your father if he had shown up in some sports car." She huffed as if she was declaring her virtue and the marriageability of my father based on his choice of wheels.

The problem with that was, I could do math. Plus, Dad had confessed at some point when I was a teenager and starting to date. Mother was right, if Dad had shown up in a sports car without a backseat, they never would have had me. I was a bit of a surprise that way. Dad confessed he thought he was going to marry Mother at some point, only my impending arrival sped that timetable up.

Did she think I still banged chicks in the back of cars? No, I had a king size bed for the seduction of my paramours.

"This is ridiculous. If adding a minivan to my collection will make you change your mind, then I will walk out of here and go to the first car dealership with some on the lot. If that's what it's going to take, I can have a van here in forty-five minutes."

"It's not the car, Alex."

No Roy, it's about power. You have it and you don't want to give it up.

"I'm aware of that. You see me as someone without focus. Someone who prioritizes fun over business. What can I do to change your perception of me?"

"Maybe if you started taking things more seriously Alexander," Mother said. "A serious relationship."

"Okay, Mom, you've got to stop." I held up both hands in a universal put on the brakes gesture. "First you want me to focus all my spare time on the business. I did that. I basically gave up five years of prime dating time to work with the product development group, so we didn't fall behind against emerging tech companies. Clearly it wasn't enough because now I'm being responsible enough and your argument is that I don't have someone lined up to start popping out babies for you?"

"Alex!"

"No, don't Alex me. When in the last five years was I supposed to find and woo a woman? I work in a primarily male industry that you wanted me to focus on."

Everyone was quiet for a long moment.

Roy cleared his throat and crossed his arms. "This is a very good example of what we are talking about Alex. You keep turning this problem back on us claiming you are doing what we asked."

"You've turned down my offer to introduce you to some good young women in town. I have connections. There are some very good families with marriageable daughters."

I closed my eyes and ran both hands through my hair. The last thing I wanted was for my mother to set me up on a date. I had to think. Would that really be so bad? It would get her off my back. No one said I had to follow through on any of those dates.

I let out a heavy breath. "Roy, you don't want this job, you never did. But you're protecting your brother's, my father's interests. I appreciate that."

I clutched at my chest, trying to convey my sincerity.

"I may not have said that before. But I do. I have this company's best interest, this family's best interest at heart. I studied computer science, and graduated top of my MBA program. I have dedicated years to ensure that we don't fall behind in the tech race. What can I do to prove that I am not some kind of fool partying my way through life? What will it take?"

I turned my stare to Red, my current personal assistant, who sat in the corner taking notes and pretending he really wasn't there. He twisted up his face and shrugged his shoulders. I rolled my eyes. This was exhausting.

"I think we would be more comfortable ceding over the company to you if we had some proof of responsibility," Roy started.

"If I agree to start dating someone?"

"I think we want something more permanent than dating."

I nodded. I hated this. If I wanted to take control over my birthright, I had two options at this point: get married or kill off my uncle. I stared hard at him for longer than I should have. Yeah, that wasn't an option.

"If you promise not to announce that I am looking to get married like one of your Regency romance movies, I will let you set me up on a date or two." I surrendered with a slight bow to Mother.

She smiled and clapped her hands. A rare smile crossed her face. I had missed seeing her smile since we lost my dad, but this really seemed like I had signed over my future.

There were a few more terms to my total surrender. I was to move out of R and D and start shadowing the CFO. If they simply wanted to restructure my role at Foundation Network Communications, why couldn't they have simply done that?

I was their puppet, and they were manipulating my strings because they could. It was all about power, and Roy loved having power over me. With a few more fake pleasantries I excused myself.

Red followed in step behind me.

I kept my mouth shut until we made it to the elevators. The doors slid shut and I turned to face the wall. I didn't trust that Roy and mom didn't review the elevator cameras when they did this to me. They would not get the pleasure of seeing me break down. At least the elevators couldn't legally have microphones in them.

"Argh," I roared in frustration as I faced the brushed steel of the elevator wall.

"A minivan?" Red practically laughed.

"Talk about a massive cock block. I need a way out of this. And we can't off Roy." I sort of laughed too.

"But you did think about it."

"Yep, right after I seriously considered buying a fucking minivan, with some baby car seats in the back for good measure. Neither of which is going to happen."

Red leaned against the elevator wall and looked at me. "Are you seriously going to date women your mother wants?"

I turned and leaned against the wall.

"I can handle a few dates with vapid, leggy models before I lose my mind." My mom had it in her head of what kind of woman my future wife needed to look like. What was so ironic was that most of the men I knew, Red included, also liked that type. Thin, elegant, poise, hip bones that stuck out in a bikini.

While I appreciated beautiful women, no matter their shape, I preferred them to have a bit of meat on their bones with handfuls of flesh I could hold onto. I liked them cute and curvy.

"Or you could just get married." Red lifted one of his brows.

I stared at him. "Go on."

"Why not do something like a mail order bride. Find someone who needs to be married, but who doesn't want to be as much as you don't."

"I think a green card situation would be a bad idea. If that went wrong, it would be handing my mom and Roy proof positive I was no good."

"Not everyone who needs to get married needs a green card."

I nodded. "Go fishing, see what you catch."

## 3

# ABIGAIL-SAM

I t was like watching a movie. I wasn't connected to my hands as I watched my fingers press the numbers. I wasn't the one doing this.

The phone rang. I hung up.

They would call me back, right?

Maybe they didn't call back numbers they didn't know. And I'm sure there were plenty of people like me calling and hanging up. Just as there were plenty of people out there who still expected someone to leave a voicemail.

My gut roiled with nerves. I dialed again. And again, as soon as it started ringing, I hung up.

I couldn't do this.

"Any luck?"

Michelle opened the door from the kitchen to the back alley. She leaned against the doorjamb and looked at me with lifted brows.

I sat on a stack of old wooden pallets the delivery company would pick up on their next delivery. I had told her that I was calling apartments on my break. Only that wasn't true. I was calling for situations listed in the classifieds of the Daily. It's where everyone from escort services to multi-level-marketing did their ads. There were roommate listings right alongside situations sought. I convinced myself I was calling both. Only I hadn't managed to complete a single call all the way through.

I shook my head in response to her query. "You know, I'm just introverted enough that I get nervous leaving voicemails. Why can't they just call me back?"

Michelle shook her head at me. "Because I'm not calling back everyone who hangs up. It's not my job to chase someone down who can't be bothered to at least let me know they are interested."

I sighed; she was right.

I absolutely hated when someone I didn't know would call, let my phone ring and hang up. Michelle was right. If I wasn't willing to call an unknown number back, these people were not going to chase me down, even if I was the perfect candidate for their situation.

Situation wanted: Single female for matrimony not marriage. No immigration. Financial compensation. Must be 21+.

I was single, over twenty-one, and in need of financial compensation. I didn't know if I was perfect or not, and I would never know if I didn't follow through.

"I'll make this call and then be right back in," I said. Michelle was being super supportive regarding my entire situation. I didn't need to take even more time away from my job. She did nothing to make me feel guilty, I just did.

"Take your time," she said before stepping back into the kitchen.

I let out a sign and dialed the number again. This time I was connected to my fingers. It wasn't someone else dialing, it was me, just as it was going to be me and not someone else leaving a message.

The phone rang. The voicemail picked up.

I listened to the entire message and in response left them all the information they wanted: my name Abigail-Samantha Cole; my age twenty-two, soon to be twenty-three; a call back number; and a brief message why I answered their ad.

"My long-term boyfriend ditched me after I paid for his tuition and rent for almost five years. Now, it was supposed to be my turn to go to school, but I'm living out of a storage unit and sleeping on my boss's couch while I look for a place to live. I have a better chance of qualifying for student aid if I'm married, same with finding a place to live. I'm originally from Alabama, but have been in Dallas for five years while my boyfriend attended UT."

I ended the call. It didn't sound like much of a sales pitch, but then again, I hadn't known what to expect. I made a quick call to a *'female roommate wanted listing'* and left a message there before going back to work.

The rest of that day was non-eventful. My phone only rang once. I love that little notification that comes up letting me know it's a likely scam. I did not answer my phone. In all honesty, I only expected if any of the calls I managed to make that day called me back, those would have been the ones looking for a roommate.

So, I was surprised when I received a voicemail from a man with a northern accent asking me to please return his call. He wanted to speak with me regarding the matrimony situation.

I told Josh I was taking a break and closed myself in Michelle's office before returning the call.

"Hello, this is Abigail-Sam, you returned my call about the classified in the Daily," I said as soon as the call connected.

"Thank you for returning my call, Abigail-Sam. You can call me Red."

Red proceeded to ask me a few questions. They seemed more like standard job application questions. Where did I see myself in five years? What had driven me to answer the ad?

"You mentioned that you've been paying for your boyfriend's rent and tuition for the past few years, why are you suddenly in need of a financial situation?"

My answer verged on too much information, but if I was expected to marry this fellow, I might as well not have anything to hide.

"I'm tired, Red. It was supposed to be my turn to not have to work, but to focus on school. I was working two jobs up until my ex-boyfriend graduated. I've been at the cafe for three years, and my boss here is great. I was gonna keep this job part-time while attending classes. But I already quit my other job. I was doing medical transcription from home."

"Why didn't you keep the work from home job instead?"

David had asked me that too when I quit.

"The work was okay, but my manager was a control freak. I think she wanted to fire me because when I quit, she actually said 'oh thank goodness.' I quit the manager more than the job, if that makes sense."

"I fully understand," Red said.

I kept talking, telling him how David was supposed to be paying rent and the utility bills, everything that had been in my name, but he hadn't. So, now I had red flags all over my records as a pay risk. If I wanted to get electricity, my deposit would be higher than if I had paid the bills late. I still owed them for a few months' worth of bills. And having an eviction on my history was making it hard to pass a credit check. What roommate or lending agent wanted to take on the financial risk of someone who was kicked out for not paying?

"So now everything costs me twice as much and I'm currently making half as much. I had to move all of my belongings into a storage unit without any notification, and moving companies charge a premium for last minute stuff like that."

"Uh, hm, and what about dating, and family plans. This is for a legally binding marriage agreement."

"First off, am I expected to be your wife?"

Red laughed for a good minute before he cleared his throat and let me know it wasn't to marry him but his boss.

"Red, to be honest, I'm burned out on men. I don't even want to date. And if your boss only needs me on paper, I'm sure being married isn't going to stop him from dating, right?"

"I have no idea, but you can safely assume that."

"So why would me being a married woman stop me from dating? Not that I want to."

"It's not the dating that's the issue here. It's the sudden need to be able to get married, should the need arise."

I let out a sigh. "Same goes for your boss, unless he's crazy old and is planning on dying while we are married."

"Not old, not dying. But he does want to set a contractual minimum time guarantee."

"So there is a time limit on this? That's good, I guess."

We talked about a few other things, nothing too memorable. No set details, vague platitudes, nothing with any kind of detail.

"What's your timeline on this?" I asked.

"When it happens, it will happen fast."

The call ended and I kicked myself for not asking if I could expect a call back, or if I should follow up in a week or so. I tried to put it out of my mind. Instead, I went off the deep end thinking about how being married for financial reasons could change everything. Red's boss sounded rich, really rich, and that this wife thing might have something to do with keeping an ex-wife from getting their hands on his money.

I panicked about money laundering, but was I setting myself up to be involved with drug money, or the mafia? Of course, I was being silly, it wasn't like I was ever going to hear from Red again.

When my phone rang less than an hour later, I expected it to be one of the roommate situations, or another scam.

But it was Red's number.

"Um, hello?"

"Miss Cole, could we meet in person?"

When I ended the call, I had an appointment to meet this Red fellow the next day. He agreed to come to the cafe, so that we were in public.

I didn't miss him the next morning. His hair was like a beacon in the dark. He had flaming orange hair. It was cut short and slicked back. The rest of his was as dashing as stylish. He oozed money.

"You must be Red," I said as soon as he stepped inside the doors. "Let me get Josh out of here so we can chat."

He looked me up and down, and then gave me the biggest smile. Either I was perfect, or the biggest 'fuck you' he could deliver. "Miss Abigail-Samantha Cole, it is a definite pleasure to meet you."

When he walked out of there an hour later, I had a ticket to Vegas and a signed contract to marry some guy named Alex a week later.

# 4

## ALEX

"Why am I putting on a tux?" I asked Red as I accepted the garment bag from him.

We were in my suite at the Bellagio in Las Vegas. I had an appointment in an hour, and I wasn't in the mood to put on brown velvet.

"You are putting on the Valentino because you are getting married. It's brown, not black because I was unable to make formal arrangements. You are going to be properly dressed for your nuptials."

"Red," I cleared my throat and prepared to snap back.

"Alex, this wedding has to be real enough for your mother to accept it. She knows you wouldn't get married in jeans and a button down. This may be a quickie Vegas wedding, but it is still a wedding."

I groaned; he was right. It made sense that I had brought a tux, and if the black one was at the cleaners, which I honestly had no idea, then I would be in the next best suit I owned. In this case that meant a velvet tux in a deep chocolate brown with silk lapels and wool silk blend trousers. I had last worn it to one of my mom's charity events.

Knowing my mom, she would recognize the suit, and assume that I had dragged it all the way to Vegas for this wedding. Thus, giving a touch of verisimilitude to the entire farce.

Red was a genius when it came to plotting this entire scenario out. I dropped hints that I had met someone even while continuing to go out with the young women that my mom selected for me. During that time, a scant three weeks, Red managed to find someone acceptable. And willing.

I announced that I was no longer willing to date other women after having met someone special. I refused any of mom's attempts to find out more about her. No names, no locations, nothing.

Of course, I didn't remember her name. It was Gail or something. Names didn't matter, and least not yet.

Now that we were in Vegas, we'd get married, have some wedding pictures taken, and then Red would concoct some tale as to why my new wife, who I was so eager to marry, would not live with me in Dallas.

"So, I'm in a suit. What about this woman? Is she going to show up in jeans and ruin the whole effect?"

I took a few steps from the living room of the suite into the bedroom. I laid the suit across the bed and started to change.

"She was given a healthy budget and told to get a wedding dress," Red assured me.

I stepped into my pants and pulled a dark cream silk shirt on. I tucked in my tails and fastened the front of the pants. Eyeballing the rest of the tux, I lifted the silk vest and held it out to Red.

"Waist coat or not?"

"Waist coat, and cream bow tie."

I shrugged into the waist coat and shoved my feet into the coordinating tapestry loafers.

"You still haven't told me about this bride of mine. What's she like, what does she even look like?"

Red stepped into the room as I stepped into the ensuite bathroom to tie up the bow around my neck.

"I think you will be pleasantly surprised. I know I was."

I raked my hand through my hair and contemplated the finer points of having not shaved while wearing a tux with a bow tie. I looked like a rake.

"How do I look?"

"Fashionably roguish. Now you know where you are going?"

"I do," I answered.

"Practice that, it's the key to your business freedom." Red joked. "I will go pick up your bride and meet you at the chapel. Don't be late."

Red clapped me on the shoulder, and then brushed off the velvet, before leaving with a chuckle.

I somehow felt that he was setting me up for a nasty surprise. My new wife would either be too old, or too supermodel kind...tall and thin. Or some semi-homeless meth addict with three teeth in her head.

He said he found someone my mother would believe. Knowing what type of girl mom wanted me to marry, I expected big hair, and a model's statuesque physique.

When I arrived at the chapel, Red was waiting for me outside.

"Are you ready?"

"Ready to be allowed access to my birthright? Ready to be finally taken seriously by my mom and Roy?" I quipped back.

"Ready to no longer be a highly sought after bachelor in Dallas?"

"Please don't tell me you bought into all of mom's romantic movie drivel. This is a business venture with a limited time scope."

"Five years is a long time," Red said.

"Only because we are standing on this side of it. In five years, this will all have passed in the blink of an eye. Is she here?"

Red nodded. "She's inside."

"Great." I brushed down the front of the velvet jacket. "What's her name again?"

"Abigail Sam—"

"That's right. Abigail, Abigail." I repeated her name a few times to get it into my head. "Here goes nothing. Wish me luck."

I stepped into the small chapel and stopped in my tracks. The chapel wasn't much more than a small room with a few rows of wooden church-style pews. There was a small wooden podium in front of a large painting of a stained-glass window. It looked like it was based on something from a French cathedral. I assumed the older man at the podium was the chaplain. An older woman sat in the very first pew—the chapel provided witness.

I turned back to see Red follow me inside. He was there as my official witness. He had a wide grin on his face.

"I told you, you would be surprised," he chuckled.

He walked past me, up to the waiting group. He said something, nodded his head and sat. I somehow managed to make note of all of that while staring at my bride.

She looked as surprised with my appearance as I was with hers. In my case, well, Red nailed it. If my mother saw a wedding photo with this woman, she would accept it was real. She wants me to be seen with a woman of a certain type, and maybe that's why I gravitated toward a different physical look.

Abigail was downright cute. She had short, blonde, hair that curled above her shoulders. Her face was sweet, soft and round, with a little peak of a chin. All of her looked soft and bountiful. I liked curves, and she had them. Her choice of dresses emphasized her breasts and skimmed over her hips. It was a nice dress, and in a champagne color. We almost coordinated.

She blinked at me with big green eyes, and then smiled. And then blushed. I realized she was younger than I had expected. But she was an adult, so she knew what she was getting into.

Hopefully I knew what I was getting into.

"Abigail," I said as I stepped up next to her.

"Abigail Sam," she said in a low voice as she looked up through her lashes at me. "Alex."

Our introduction was as simple as it could be. And then the chaplain began. I didn't pay much attention, and he kept everything brief. It was pretty much over before it started, and then he said I could kiss the bride.

Abigail giggled as I bent over to kiss her. Her lips were soft and supple. I could have been convinced to keep kissing her some more, but the old lady was clearing her throat as if we were being indecent.

"Congratulations Alex, Abigail. We need to take some pictures, and then there's some paperwork for you."

That's when I noticed she was holding a camera and had snapped us smooching.

Abigail muttered her name again. Maybe she was nervous. Maybe she was reminding herself that she wanted to keep her maiden name even though she was now a married woman.

We posed for photos and didn't really have much of a chance to talk while the older woman bustled us around the chapel, and then out into the small office to sign the papers. The entire time she kept saying things about how we looked so coordinated.

I had my suspicion that Red had arranged that somehow. It was over almost as soon as it began. We stood in front of the chapel looking at each other awkwardly.

"This is where I leave you for the evening. You have reservations at L'Atelier at the MGM. After that you are on your own. Alex, I have extended your hospitality to Abigail—"

"Abigail-Sam," she interrupted.

"Stone, if you decide to take my last name," I said.

Red continued, "She will fly back to Dallas with us in the jet. After that you can officially get on with the rest of your lives."

A long black limo pulled in front of the chapel. Red opened the back door. "This is your ride, champagne on ice is inside. Enjoy your honeymoon." He winked at me.

He knew my honeymoon was going to last through dinner, and then maybe some drinks, and then back to my suite alone.

Red helped Abigail into the back of the limo, and I walked around to climb in from the other side.

"So," she started as I climbed into the car. "You're Alex. Nice to meet you."

"Nice to meet you, too." I reached for the bottle of bubbly and popped it open.

Abigail let out a little gasp and then giggled.

I poured her a glass and handed it over. "I don't know about you, but I think tonight, after dinner, we should hit the casino and maybe take in a show. We look entirely too good to shuffle back to our rooms without being seen."

She held her glass out and I touched it with mine. "We do look good. And that sounds like fun."

# 5

## ABIGAIL-SAM

My husband was hot. There was really no other way to describe the man. He was tall and had the kind of classic bone structure that meant he'd be good looking no matter his age or his physique. His thick, dark hair had just enough curl that he probably looked super sexy when he was going with a scruffy look.

But tonight, he wasn't scruffy, he was yummy. Super yummy. I don't know if dinner was or not. It was posh. The portions were tiny, and I kept drinking champagne and staring at Alex and not eating. At some point the dashing bow tie had come off, and he undid the first few buttons of his shirt.

He was super star drool-worthy sexy. And that was one hell of a self-esteem problem. Sexy men like him, tall, dreamy, jacked, didn't like soft squish like I had. I didn't enjoy my dinner because I was too nervous to eat around him.

Over the past five years, I hadn't been aware of most of David's flaws. I brushed away the red flags of our relationship as quirks and uncomfortable truths. Being a big curvy girl was one of those uncomfortable truths. Well, uncomfortable, because David felt it was his place to remind me how much I was eating. As if I wasn't aware that if I was to be seen with him, I was not to take more than a nibble of anything other than a good healthy salad. And I don't think David had ever seen the inside of a gym.

Alex clearly worked out. And there were no leafy green options on the menu. So, I let him order for us both, and I drank more champagne.

Dinner turned into gambling. Alex kept winning. His joy made me smile. Having a perfect man like him smiling at me made me giddy. Or maybe that was the champagne.

"You are my good luck charm tonight, Abigail." He kissed me. It was a meaningless press of the lips. He then took a hand full of the chips he had just won and tucked them into the cleavage of my dress.

"Abigail-Sam," I corrected and giggled as he kept putting the coin shaped chips between my breasts, like I was some kind of slot machine. I think he was a little tipsy as well.

"Wife," he said instead of trying to say my name properly.

After another big win, he kissed me again. Only this time it wasn't a press of lips. There was a slide, and a pause, and a tasting of my lower lip. Placing his hands to hold my face he continued to taste and nibble.

I bit his lower lip, bringing it between my own. As I kissed him back, his arms wrapped around me and pulled me against his chest. For a fleeting moment I noticed how hard his body felt pressed against mine. But I didn't hold that thought for long. Soon I couldn't think.

His tongue slid alongside mine. He held the back of my neck, keeping me against him. His arms tightened like bands. I was in his grasp and going nowhere.

When the kiss ended, there were no words. His eyes were heated as he looked at me.

I could hardly breathe with the flames that had engulfed my entire being with his touch. I wanted to be bold, I wanted to ask my husband if he wanted to play the honeymoon gig with me. After that kiss I didn't know if I could handle the rejection. It was bad enough I was married to someone so far out of my league for the price of rent and tuition.

I blinked back tears as it hit me. The only way I was ever going to get a gut like him was this way, under false pretenses. I had thought I didn't want another man in my life for a very long time, and then Alex Stone went and kissed me like that.

"Your room or mine?" His voice was so low and husky, I didn't think I had heard him properly.

I blinked, this time to clear all those stupid thoughts from my brain.

"I have a view of the fountain from my room. You want to see it?"

A blink later and we were across the casino, through the lobbies and taking the elevators up to the hotel rooms. Alex practically dragged me down the hall when I gave him my room number. I handed him my card key, and then we were in the room, and I was back in his arms.

Our lips crashed together. I ran my hands over the broad expanse of his chest. He pulled his suit jacket off, and I unfastened the buttons of his vest. He took over undoing the buttons of his shirt as I worked on his belt.

I turned and presented my back and zipper. My dress, which had been almost the exact color of his shirt, fell to the floor. I turned and Alex was on his knees peeling my foundation garments down. Casino chips flew everywhere as my bra came off.

I giggled, but Alex growled as he looked at me, and palmed my breasts in his large hands. He grabbed at my rounded parts as if he couldn't touch me enough. I felt worshiped. We climbed onto the bed, touching each other, kissing. His actions were as desperate as I was.

I wanted his skin against mine. I wanted him to surround me, to take me.

Alex pressed me back against the mattress. His mouth descended onto one of my breasts. He licked and teased my nipple until it peaked hard with need. I writhed with need as he sucked and kissed across my middle. He spread my thighs and began kissing the soft skin of my inner thigh, working his way up from my knee toward my core.

I twisted my fingers into his hair, and gasped as his mouth worked its magic over me. There was no going slow. This was hot and greedy. Alex was there to take what he wanted. I was more than willing to be the object that he fulfilled his lusts with.

I cried out when his tongue, cool and surprising, licked my slit, and slid between the folds of my pussy. That man did not need a map to find my clit. He knew exactly what and where to suck.

There was no thinking. There was only Alex between my legs, and the way my body responded. There was no conscious effort to rock my hips against his face. Everything I did was instinctive and reflexive.

If I thought about what I was doing, what I needed to do I would have frozen up. But my body took its lead from him.

He played with my body like I had been his toy for a very long time. He knew all the right buttons to lick and suck and stroke. I felt my nerves bunching and tightening. Just when I thought he was going to take me over the edge he pulled away and climbed back up my body.

I opened my eyes, and his gaze locked with mine. He had a wicked grin on his face. He knew exactly what he was doing to me, and he seemed to be enjoying himself in the playground of my body. His fingers bit into my leg as he lifted my hip into position, and then he slid into me.

I gasped. The orgasm his actions had herded me toward loomed large on the horizon. I ground my heels into the bed and bucked for him. His thrusts were hard and heavy. I didn't think I had even been loved like this before. There was something beyond physical about what he was doing to me.

I screamed as I lost all sense, and the orgasm sucked me under like a riptide. It was intense and all encompassing. Alex's yell mingled with mine before he fell around me.

He didn't say anything. He kissed me with a happy hum, rolled off the bed and vanished into the bathroom. When he returned to the bed, he grabbed the open bottle of champagne I had started before I left for the wedding. He took a drink and then handed me the bottle.

"Ready for more?" he asked as I took a swig from the bottle.

I was too poleaxed to speak. I nodded, and barely had time to put the bottle down before he was dragging my ankles and pulling me down the bed.

We didn't get much sleep.

Light from the open curtains let us know it was morning. With a groan Alex rolled up and swung his legs over the side of the bed. I really wanted to reach out and caress his skin one last time. But his groans were not the sound of someone resistant to get out of bed. I knew the sound well. It rattled through my brain as well. It was the sound of 'what the hell had I done last night?' and "just how much did I drink?'

I watched Alex through mostly closed lids.

He glanced back at me and winced. That was a shot right through my ego. Screw him.

I sat up. "Are you leaving so soon?"

He grunted as he pulled on his clothes. "The plane will be ready at eleven. You still have your airline ticket, right?"

"I do?" Why did he need to know that? Red had invited me back on the private jet.

"You'll need it." He fished out his wallet from his inner jacket pocket. Peeling off several hundred dollar bills he tossed them onto the bed. "That should take care of your expenses for the day."

He turned, paused, and then faced me again. "Don't come to the airfield. Take your first-class flight home."

I stared at the money on the sheet and then up at him. I grabbed a few of the bills and held them up.

"What the hell is this for? I'm not some prostitute."

He stepped away from me and opened the door.

"No Abigail, you're my wife. You're more expensive."

With a roar of anger, I hurled the money at him as he stepped out of my room. The door closed behind him. "My name is Abigail-Sam you asshole."

# 6

# ALEX

"Congratulations on your retirement!" I stood and greeted my uncle and mom as they joined me at the table. I arranged for them to meet me for lunch. Small appetizers and champagne were already placed, waiting for their arrival.

"What are you talking about?" Mom asked.

I helped her into her chair and gave Roy a hearty handshake.

"What's going on here Alex?"

I took my seat and popped open the champagne. "I am following up on your promise to allow me to finally step into my role taking over the company."

"Alexander, your uncle made no such promise."

I clenched my jaw and exposed my teeth in a smile a shark would be proud of. "But he did. And you were there, so was my personal manager. And you agreed to the terms. If I got married, Roy would step down."

"If, Alexander, only if but you stopped dating any of the young ladies I introduced you to," Mother pointed out.

Roy snorted through his nose and crossed his arms. He was not happy with me. I didn't care. If they thought they could throw roadblocks in my way, it wasn't my fault that I found a way to move those blocks out of the way.

I nodded and didn't reply. I picked up my menu and glanced over the offerings. "I understand this place has excellent grilled salmon. I thought you would appreciate that, Mom. You've mentioned that you are trying to cut out red meat. Don't worry Roy, they also have an excellent wagyu rib eye. That's what I'll be getting. After all, we are here to celebrate."

Mother huffed. Roy grumbled. I enjoyed their discomfort and disappointment a little too much. Once I provided the evidence they had hounded me over, if they continued to deny me, I was prepared to call in a team of lawyers and sue my own mother and uncle for attempting to steal my company.

I had played the game their way for too long. It was time to take back what was rightfully mine. And if I had to resort to— what I knew they would consider— underhanded tactics, then so be it.

I continued to act as if nothing was out of the ordinary. I chatted about inane topics and ordered an excessively elaborate lunch with lobster tail bisque and the aforementioned steak. If they had gold-foiled quail eggs on the menu, I would have ordered those as well.

I was trying to get a point across. I could play their games, I could live my preferred lifestyle, and I could still win. This lunch wasn't to celebrate a retirement, or a marriage. It was my victory lap.

"Okay, Alex, we can see that you are trying to make a point. Why don't you come forth with it already," Roy said.

"I would think it was fairly obvious. I have congratulated you on your impending retirement, based on the contingencies you put forth you should have extrapolated that I should be congratulated on getting married."

"But you aren't married, son," he said.

The rage that filled me would have exploded light bulbs if I hadn't kept it under control. It wasn't the first time since my father's death Roy had called me that.

"I am not your son," I hissed through clenched teeth.

Mother gasped in shock. "Alexander!"

I paused, pasted a sharp grimace on my face and took a long moment to compose myself. I downed the rest of my champagne, filled the flute again, and drained that as well. After what felt like a very long, very tense silence I let out a long breath.

"Roy, I'm aware that you have stepped in to fill a void my father left. However, in some cases it hasn't been necessary. I have been capable of running my father's business for years. I have deferred to your judgement and adhered to your requirements."

I lifted the case that had been leaning against the legs of my chair onto my lap. The latches clicked as I opened them. I removed a file folder and handed it across the table to him. After placing the case back on the floor, I turned my attention to mom.

"I am married, Mother. I told you that I met someone who suited me much better than any of those other women you had set me up with."

My gut clenched as thoughts of Abigail and her soft body and wanton moans ricocheted through my head. With a simple classified ad and pure luck, Red had located a woman more to my liking than my mother had in years of trying to set me up. Not once had she asked me what I liked in a woman. She always found someone who looked the way she had always wanted a daughter to look. She never paid attention to what I was attracted to.

I didn't know my wife well. Hell, I didn't know her at all, but what I knew of her, she had a greater ambition and sense of purpose than being the wife of a rich man.

A chuckle escaped my lips. And of all the women, the one who's life goal wasn't to marry a rich man was the one who had.

"What are we looking at?" Roy handed my mother the file folder after he glanced at the documents within.

Mother pulled out one of the wedding portraits. Her face went through a variety of expressions, landing on confusion before she looked up at me. Holding out the photo she asked, "Who is this woman? What is this, Alexander?"

I took the photo, reached out and took the folder. "That is my wife, Abigail. Isn't she lovely? I told you I had met someone and that I wasn't interested in dating the daughters of your friends. Last weekend we decided to elope. We both knew what we wanted, and it didn't seem worth it to drag the whole engagement process out."

"You're married? I don't believe you." Mother huffed and crossed her arms.

"Alex, we're done playing this game, whatever it is," Roy growled.

"This game," I said as I pulled out a copy of my marriage certificate and displayed it for them to see, "is over. You required that I be married before you conceded to retire and hand over the company that is rightfully mine. I am legally married, and to a woman who I find to be quite adorable."

There was no lie in my words. Abigail was cute, curvy, and blonde. If it weren't for our particular arrangement, had I met her on my own I probably would have pursued her until I grew bored with her.

Mom sighed. "You have always preferred girls with bigger..." her words trailed off. She wasn't going to say anything about Abigail's larger hips or beasts, even though that is what she was thinking. "I can see how you would be attracted to her. If you are married, then why isn't she here? Why aren't you introducing us to your wife?"

"She's not here because she had to be home taking care of her family. She also doesn't like the city. I plan on spending my weekends with her for the time being as we figure out exactly what the living arrangements will be." I lied. I had no intention of spending time with my wife, and we knew exactly what the living arrangements were. She lived her life the way she wanted, where she wanted, and I would do the same.

"I'm not to know my daughter-in-law?"

"She is a very private woman. I expect you to respect that."

My attention was drawn to the arrival of our meals. I tucked the documents away, sliding the folder back into my case. I was glad for the distraction of the food.

"Oh, look, our lunch has arrived."

"Alex, what do you think you are getting away with?" Roy said in a low voice as a plate full of aromatic steak was set in front of me.

"I'm not getting away with anything Roy. But I do have witnesses to your claim that you will step down and retire when I am married. I'm married. Legally and biblically, don't be so crude as to ask me to prove that I have bedded my wife. I have proven time and again that not only am I willing to meet your requirements to prove that I am capable of the job, but I have also gone above and beyond. Legally, I could have pushed at any point, but I didn't because I believed you were acting in the best interest of the business and our family. But you have been dragging this out, finding new excuses at every turn, just like dad. You two are very similar. Don't make the same mistake he did."

I took a bite of my steak. It was flavorful and practically melted in my mouth. Totally worth the hundred dollars cut. I closed my eyes and enjoyed the food for a moment.

"Wouldn't you rather go out and enjoy the life you can now afford, or do you really want to work until you die at your desk?"

Mom sobbed and rushed from the table.

I watched her leave. I didn't feel an inkling of guilt for upsetting her. My father had died at his desk. It was a life choice I saw no merit in.

"Now look at what you've done," Roy growled. He stood and tossed his napkin on the table while glaring at me.

"Congratulations on your retirement, Roy," I said.

His eyes went wide, and his shoulders slumped before he stormed off. I think he got my point. I took another bite of the steak. It really was so very good.

# 7

## SAMMY

*ix years later...*

There was a light knock on my office door. I looked up and saw my Vice President, Vanessa Marche, hovering. She had started off as a friend and assistant, but her insights into business were so valuable, I quickly realized that her time was wasted being my assistant.

As usual, Vanessa was perfectly dressed in stylish vintage inspired office wear. Her ability to accessorize was so spot on I frequently wondered why she wasn't working in the fashion industry instead of working with me in the tech industry.

"Do you read the Dallas Daily, Sammy?"

"Of course." Didn't everyone? It was the quintessential gossip and events newspaper in town. "We got our start advertising in the back."

"Yeah, but do you pay attention to the articles or just the announcements about upcoming events?"

I had a weird personal connection with the Daily. I secretly credited it with helping me be the woman I was today. After all, it's how I met my husband.

"I don't know if you read this yet"— Vanessa dropped a copy of the magazine-like newspaper on my desk— "but I think we need to take the invitation to MTC Expo seriously."

I picked up the Daily and I didn't sigh. I didn't stare longingly at the handsome man poised on the cover. Instead, I flipped the paper over and glanced at the classifieds, and thumbed backward until I reached the article.

There was another photo of Alex Stone. This time I did sigh. Only Vanessa would never know the real reason. I scanned the article.

Party boy, businessman, enigma around town, frequently seen with celebrity dates, and gorgeous models, never seen to actually have a romantic interest in anyone. Why did business articles about Alex always have to include at least one paragraph speculating about his personal life?

I knew exactly why he was seen with hot models, because his wife didn't give two shakes. No, that wasn't true. I gave shakes, many shakes. And, later when no one was around I would shake the paper because I couldn't do anything to him.

The morning after our nuptials, and the best sex of my life, he walked out. I hadn't seen him in person since. I avoided going to conferences if he was a presenter. And I stayed away from Foundation Network Communications as best as I could.

"We are small potatoes in personal networking. Stone wouldn't waste his time with us." I was convinced that was the case.

Alex always went after bigger fish in smaller ponds. We were a small fish in a local puddle when it came to market share. If Foundation Network Communications came after us, we wouldn't even be able to bite back— they were too big, and we couldn't open our corporate mouth wide enough to sink our teeth in.

"I wouldn't be so certain about that." Vanessa turned the page and put her finger on a pull quote. Her perfectly manicured red nail traced a path my eyes followed.

'We are looking to branch out into more niche markets.'

"He wants to expand into areas that were not on his radar before. Do you still think we are too small to be of interest to the big boys now?"

I looked up at her. She had her lips quirked to the side, and her eyes wide behind the bright red heart-shaped rim of her glasses. I trusted her judgement better than my own.

When I started Eyes On Care, a babysitting exchange and nanny finding networking platform, it was out of desperation. After a year and a half of taking classes and working part time at the cafe, Michelle, my boss, my mother by choice, fired me and then left me. I knew her abandonment wasn't personal. She didn't have a choice.

I hoped her real daughter knew just how incredibly lucky she was. For something as awful as it was, the timing couldn't have been more synchronous. Michelle was looking to sell the coffee shop, and her daughter's husband had just died in a car accident. Michelle left Dallas to go take care of her daughter and grandchildren across the country during a very sad time in their lives.

I hadn't actually been fired. I only kept the job because I felt as if I owed Michelle so much. Thanks to Alex, I had a very nice arrangement that covered my tuition and expenses, and paid for a small, but very nice condo. While I felt left abandoned once Michelle left, I knew I wasn't.

I knew what real abandonment was. I experienced the fear of not knowing if Mom was coming back in a day or a week. Would she be alone or with a new man? I knew how to make a few dollars in change, dug out of the couch, or found it on the sidewalk, and turned it into a week's worth of food. It was better if she left during the week, I'd only have to scrounge for dinner, thanks to school lunches. But the weekends she took off were harder. Sometimes I wondered if I had a sister or a brother, would Mom have stayed around more?

She was why I latched onto David so hard, and why his betrayal hurt. No, Michelle hadn't abandoned me. But I did miss her. Without her, I desperately needed someone to watch Xander while I attended classes.

Campus had a very small childcare center, and they couldn't guarantee a place for Xander. Eyes On Care was started as a flier on the center's bulletin board. It then grew to a page on a popular social media platform.

After a year of operation, Vanessa stepped in and said we should make our own platform. We were both computer science majors. Between us we had the programming skills to create what we needed. And when we didn't, we hired a programmer, Brad.

Vanessa helped to launch Eyes On Care into what it is now, so I trusted her. If she said we needed to start paying attention to what Alex Stone was doing, then I needed to pay attention to what my husband was up to.

This time when I sighed, it had nothing to do with memories of Alex Stone.

"Okay, what exactly does MTC Expo think they can do for us?"

Vanessa proceeded to lay out how Eyes On Care could leverage from the conference by approaching Foundation Network Communications. Her suggestion was instead of playing chase, running away from the bigger company, and building a defense, was to go after them. Put ourselves in their path and see what kind of offer they could come up with.

This would put us in the offensive position. Give us the upper hand.

"Do we want to put a proposal together now before we bait the hook, or do we wait for them to bite first?"

Vanessa slid into the chair opposite my desk. "I think we need to brainstorm and come up with a handful of ways they might want to take us on. And then we have contingency proposals for each scenario. If all they want is to buy us out and shut us down, we make a plan for that. If they want to absorb us and integrate our tech into their platforms, we make a plan."

"And if they want to buy us out and keep us running, do we have a plan for that?" I asked.

"Exactly. Ideally, they buy us out and expand us into markets faster than we can grow ourselves, and that should be our primary focus."

I scanned the article again. "But it doesn't say that Foundation Network Communications is actively taking over any businesses."

Vanessa shrugged. "Not at the moment. But Alex does mention that it's the direction he wants to go in. So, we should get in his way, make him notice us."

My gut clenched. I didn't know if I actually wanted Alex Stone's attention. The last time I had his attention, it hadn't gone exactly as planned. Even so, I was doing pretty well without it.

"What if we're prepared for all scenarios but they don't even look at us?" Something that could very well happen, and I wouldn't be opposed to.

Vanessa grinned, wide and toothy, like a very pretty shark. She hadn't wasted her time in the Computer Science department, and after a semester of working with me developing Eyes On Care, she double majored in business.

"If they aren't interested, we still will have proposals in place. With a little rearranging of the information and graphs we have everything we need to go out and collect investors. It's a win-win no matter what, because we are positioning ourselves to be the ones in charge of any kind of interest. If nothing else, this is an excuse to finally get play-books created for a variety of business scenarios we should be prepared for."

"Thinking ahead," I replied.

"Proactive, not reactive," she responded.

I might have started the business out of desperation, but today we were thinking ahead that got us where we are. When Vanessa, Brad, Cindy, a second programmer, and I all graduated, we already had lucrative jobs. And as a matter of fact, Eyes On Care was doing so well at that time it had been a very real temptation to not finish college at all. But thinking ahead, we completed our graduation as a contingency plan for employment. And here we were two years later, more successful than any of us could have imagined because I needed a babysitter and offered to swap sitting services with other student mothers.

# 8

## ALEX

I reviewed my calendar for the week. I knew I had a handful of meetings scheduled and wanted to be certain to go over the right notes. Nothing conveyed ineptitude more than talking to a tech firm about leveraging their product into the completely wrong market. With so many back-to-back meetings, I really had to be on top of my notes. I was not going to show up at a meeting not knowing who I was meeting with or what their product was.

There was a list of company names for the meetings. I had a stack of file folders with briefs on each company. First on my schedule was something called GIFU.com, I confirmed that their file folder was at the top of my stack. Next on my schedule was Eyes On Care, but I didn't see a file or any notes on them. I had nothing.

"Call Harper," I barked at my phone.

"Calling Harper McKinnon," a smooth computerized voice responded.

"Alex, what can I do for you?" Harper's voice came through the phone intercom system.

"I have a meeting with Eyes On Care tomorrow. There are no notes. Who are these people and why am I the one meeting them?"

"Let me see what I can dig up." There was silence as she ended the call.

I flipped through the folder on GIFU.com, a small mobile networking company providing delivery services. GIFU.com. It was an unfortunate acronym. They were local. If they were any good at what they did, they could easily expand into other areas. I made a few notes on stickies and began looking over their website. For a company with .com in their name, their site was a mess. Their user interface was horrible. I pulled out some more facts on them.

My phone began vibrating a second before the ringtone, and then the voice announcing Roy was on the line.

"Answer phone," I said to the smart device.

"Alex," Roy's voice filled my office.

I may have grimaced. I had barely managed to force him into retirement over five years ago, but that hadn't stopped him from inserting himself back into my business. "Why aren't you in the Maldives, or some place exotic like that?" I asked.

"Who said I'm not?" he chuckled.

"The fact that you are calling is a dead giveaway." I shut down the bad website I had been looking at, scrawled a large NO on a sticky note, and slapped it on top of the GIFU.com folder. That was an hour and a half I could have saved myself from. I'd pass the meeting on to someone else, and if they thought they could resurrect the mess that company wanted to present us with, then they would have to be able to justify the time and expense. As far as I was concerned, GIFU.com, and Roy, could go elsewhere and stop bothering me.

Unfortunately, that was not an option.

"How's that expansion directive being handled?"

I closed my eyes and let out a heavy breath. He no longer could stake a claim to be involved in the day to day running of my business. As a fixture within the board, he was perfectly able to oversee what was going on. If I had my way, I would have had him removed from the board as well. I didn't like his fingers digging into my work.

I had thought I scored a major coup when I ran off and got married. All Roy and Mother said it would take to trust me was getting married. That had not been the truth of it.

Not by half. Roy had retired, but only after several months of infighting, and threatening to walk away with the people who made up Foundation Network Communications. He could keep the servers, he could keep the proprietary programming, but without the people, there was nothing, and that's when he finally caved.

Caved, but not relented.

"I'll fill you in at the next board meeting," I said through clenched teeth.

He let out a hearty laugh. "Alex, you can share that with me now."

I wasn't joking. "I don't have time to review everything with you, Roy, not when you will receive a more detailed report next week at the board meeting."

"You know I like to know what to expect, so there are no surprises during the actual meeting."

"Roy, I have a business to run. You are sent an agenda before every meeting. Next week will be no different."

"Call from Harper McKinnon," the smart device announced.

"Goodbye, Roy, end call." I gave the smart device the necessary instructions and Harper's voice was the next thing I heard.

"I have the information you wanted. Thomas met them at the MTC Expo. He seems pretty impressed with them. They are a childcare networking platform, they fit with our overarching strategy. And he thinks you will be impressed also. Your meeting is with Sammy Cole and Vanessa Marche first thing tomorrow."

"That gives me something to work with. Do me a favor and if Thomas isn't available, find someone who can be there for the meeting with GIFU.com. I need our guys to sit through their presentation and then assess if they think it's worth pursuing."

"Sounds like you've made up your mind already," she laughed.

"I'm not saying anything. I don't want to influence someone else's opinion."

She laughed some more before ending the call.

I immediately looked up Eyes On Care. Without a registration and login, I couldn't see how their platform functioned. But the introductory page, and the about section of their website was highly informative.

It wasn't going to take a huge brainstorming session to figure out how working together with Eyes On Care would be beneficial to both. I jotted down my thoughts. As much as I liked the voice command for the smart device to answer my phone, I still had problems with voice to text transcription. Far too often I would look at a string of words and wonder what the hell I had said.

A quick search on Sammy Cole gave me a slew of generic information, but nothing more personal than his initials A.S. And Vanessa Marche's information looked a lot like a social media influencer hit the tech world. She was not only the VP of the company, but apparently the face as well.

I did my homework so that the following morning I was prepared.

Or so I thought.

None of my research prepared me for the women who walked into the conference room to meet with me. It was my own bias regarding tech firms. Of course, a company making childcare easier would have been the brain-child of women. So why had I expected Sammy to be a man?

"Mr. Stone, thank you for meeting with us. Is your colleague Thomas joining us?" Vanessa was just as she appeared in all of her photos. Groomed with a heavy flair of vintage style, and a penchant for bright red.

When I looked past her at the other woman, I swallowed and tried to remember who Thomas was.

Sammy Cole stood slightly behind Vanessa, clearly allowing the other, recognizable woman to take the lead. She was subtle in contrast to Vanessa's bright colors and forthright attitude.

Sammy Cole wore muted tones and high-end designer clothes. Her dark hair was pulled away from her face but fell in languorous waves past her shoulders. And her eyes, sharp and bright, caught everything behind sensible frames.

It only took a few seconds after meeting her to know I was a goner. I stood no chances of being coherent after I took in the rest of her. She was sex appeal on legs. Something about her was familiar, like I had known her my entire life.

"It's a pleasure to meet you both. Would you like something to drink? Coffee?" I stumbled over the thoughts in my head, fortunately my words were smooth.

"No, but thank you," Sammy answered.

Her voice was intoxicating. I needed someone else in this meeting immediately. Not that I didn't know how to behave around attractive women. I was suddenly overwhelmed by this particular one in a way that I couldn't say I had experienced before. I needed backup simply so that I didn't forget something important during the meeting.

"Let me see if Thomas will be joining us," I said as an excuse to step out of the conference room.

I turned the corner and pushed my way into an empty break room and hit Harper's number.

"Shouldn't you be in a meeting right now?"

"Yeah." I paused for a second figuring out what I should say. I couldn't say 'Send help. I'm an adult man and I'm reacting to this woman like a sex starved teenager. This woman's presence is going to kill me.' That was unprofessional and completely sexist, even if it was true.

"I think this presentation needs a second pair of eyes on it. I don't want to miss anything. Are you or Thomas available?"

"Thomas is with the F-U people. He keeps texting me, apparently, they are a real mess, and you owe him one. I'm working remotely today. Go back to your meeting, I will have someone there in ten minutes or less."

"Harper, you're a God send."

"I'll remind you of that when it's time for a raise." She ended the call.

I returned to the conference with the same excuse I had given Harper. I thought a second pair of eyes on their presentation was warranted.

Less than ten minutes later, Thomas burst into the conference room. "I am so sorry I made you wait. I'm glad Alex called me in. I'm really looking forward to this after what we talked about at the expo."

It didn't take long into the presentation before I was drawn into their vision of how Foundation Network Communications would benefit from a partnership with them. I tucked my rabid attraction to their CEO aside and was even more impressed with the insider information on how their company started, which wasn't published on the website. This woman was brilliant.

As if she needed to be even more perfect than I already thought her to be.

## 9

# SAMMY

I didn't know how I was managing to pull this off, but I was. No one knew that Alex Stone and I had a history. Including him.

At first, I thought for certain he was going to stop our initial presentation and call me out. I expected him to turn to me and ask me what I thought I was doing there. But he didn't. And, in the follow up emails during the past one week, he didn't seem to recognize me as well. Not a single message calling me Abigail or hinting that we had a situation.

I knew I had changed, but had it really been that much? My hair was longer, and I stopped bleaching it. Having a kid had shifted my shape around a bit. My hips were wider, but I had started off with curves and extra padding.

Even if Alex did know who I was, he acted as if he didn't. Assuming he had his reasons, I wasn't going to announce my presence as his wife. And if he flat out asked me why I didn't say anything, I'd figure out something when the time came.

I was already stressed with having to go meet with him on my own. Alone with Alex Stone was a potentially dangerous situation. Of course, this was a business meeting and alcohol would not be involved.

I parked and sat in my car for a moment. I sighed as I pulled the tote with my laptop onto my lap.

"You've got this," I said to myself in the pull-down mirror in the visor. I ran a dusty peach lipstick over my lips. Unlike Vanessa, who only ever wore red lipstick, I only wanted a touch of color so that I didn't look as tired as I felt.

Cool air rolled over me as I stepped into the building. "I have a meeting with Alex Stone," I said to the receptionist.

"Take the elevators up to the tenth floor, I'll let them know to expect you."

Tenth floor? That had to be his office. When Vanessa and I had come for the presentation, we had been taken to a conference room on the second floor. Nerves danced through my entire body as the elevator doors closed and it started to lift.

The doors opened with a ding, and I stepped out.

"Sammy."

I swallowed hard. There was something entirely too right the way Alex said my name. An involuntary giggle escaped my lips as I thought about how he couldn't get my name right when I was using the short version of my given name Abigail-Sam. I think he actually thought Sam was my last name.

I ditched the overly complicated name after I got married. I was no longer the girl who had latched onto a narcissist to escape a negligent home life. David had been overly formal. I came to realize that it was his way of acting and presenting himself as being more important than anyone else. If someone used contractions, he refused. As if it somehow made him look better.

Growing up, my mother only ever used my full name Abigail-Samantha Teresa Cole when I was in trouble. Sammy had been my name for most of my life, and then I met David. He had made such a big deal being the one who converted me into using my full name like a proper adult. Being with David had made me feel like a grown up.

I was the adult in our relationship. I paid the bills; I took on the responsibilities. And when I was done with him, I was done with that name that had always been such a pain to write, and to get people to say.

Returning to Sammy as my name of choice felt like returning to myself. The concept of going home and feeling relaxed and at peace was a foreign concept to me. Home had never been a place of safety I would want to return to. But being my authentic self, I totally understood that.

And having Alex call me by my name, I knew what it felt like when planets aligned, and angels sang.

I turned and smiled at him.

"You don't mind if I call you Sammy, do you?" He held out his hand.

It was warm as it wrapped around my fingers. It was best if I pushed down the memories of what his hands had done to me.

"It's my name. Why would I mind?" My stomach dropped, was he going to call my bluff and ask why didn't I go by Abigail?

"You can call me Alex."

I made a big deal of wiping my forehead. "Oh, good. Since that's what I've been writing in the emails all week. Imagine how embarrassed I would be if your name was Kent?"

"Kent?" His lips twitched to the side in a half grin.

I shrugged, and panicked, it was the first name I could think of. "Don't tell me your name is really Kent?"

He shook his head. "Not at all. Shall we?" He held out his arm indicating the direction I needed to start walking in.

We passed a large polished blond maple desk, and then he led me through into his office. My office looked nothing like the lap of luxury in which he conducted business. This was the kind of large space with floor to ceiling windows that movie makers always put CEO's in.

They were never shown in a small office about the size of an office cubicle, with windows that looked out onto the rest of the office workers. Offices like that were always saved for middle management or detectives on TV. That's what my office looked like, with generic cream-colored walls and beige fixtures. Alex's office was on a completely different financial and style level than mine.

I headed to the cluster of chairs and a low table in the middle of the office. My other option was to head toward his desk. Sitting across his desk while I presented numbers would feel entirely too much, like being in trouble and seeing the school principal.

"Drink?" Alex asked as I took a seat and began unpacking my laptop.

"Water, thank you."

He waved a glass in his hand at me. "Put that away. I can look at numbers in an email. I want to talk to you, get a feel of the business."

"Isn't that what the numbers will do?"

He handed me a tall glass with ice cubes and water before taking a seat in the chair next to me. Not across from me. He was entirely too close for my personal comfort.

I twisted so that I could look at him. "Should I go ahead and email you this presentation and the spreadsheets?"

"That would be good." He sat back and stretched his arms across the backs of the chairs.

The hair on my arms stood on end as a tingle traveled over them and up the back of my neck. I shivered.

Alex reached out and touched my arm. "You're cold, I'll adjust the AC."

"Oh, don't bother. I'm fine. Just a random chill."

"If you say so. Now, Sammy, tell me about you and how did someone like you come up with Eyes On Care?"

"Really?" I bit the inside of my cheek as I realized I was suddenly very comfortable around him, to the point of being slightly flippant. "Of all the things to ask. The company's history is on our About page. I know you read everything you could find on us before our first meeting."

"You know this?" His brow furrowed and his eyebrows arched.

I laughed. "You didn't get where you are without researching the companies you invite in for presentations. Just like I did the research on you. After all, it was a random article where you were quoted as wanting to expand into niche markets that sparked the idea that has me here."

"You seem to know more about me than I do of you."

He honestly had no idea.

"Let me take you out to dinner. Give me a chance to get to know you."

I froze and then gulped. Alex Stone had just asked me out. Not a date, business.

"Do you invite other CEOs out to dinner to get to know them better?" I teased. I bit my lip as my gaze dropped from his eyes to his lips.

I remembered those lips all too well. He licked his lip ever so slightly, showing the tip of his tongue. Before I allowed myself the extravagance of ogling him, I forced my eyes back up to meet his. But the damage was already done. He had been very aware of how I lingered over his mouth.

A knowing smirk spread his lips into a very sexy grin. "Say yes," he demanded. His voice rumbled in his chest.

"You didn't answer my questions, Alex."

"I have been known to have business dinners before. Having dinner with you is something that I think should matter greatly to the two of us."

My gut clenched; this was it. He was going to announce that he knew who I was at dinner. I froze my smile in place. I didn't need him to know I was actually afraid of what he might do once our little secret was out.

"I will have dinner with you. Will we be joined by anyone else? After all, this is a business dinner," I relented.

He shook his head ever so slightly. "Will that be a problem?"

The challenge in his eyes was very clear. Hell yes, it was going to be a problem. How did he expect me to focus on business when I would spend half the time terrified that he would announce he knew who I was and that there was no possible way our businesses could find a way to work together? And then there was what I would be spending the other half of my time doing, mooning over the man who was technically my husband. He was a complete stranger who I had come to admire from afar, and I found him to be irresistibly attractive.

I should definitely say this was a problem in the making. "No problem at all. I look forward to continuing our discussion over dinner."

## 10

## ALEX

"Reservation for Stone," I said as I strode into Lottie's.

The maître d' confirmed and asked if I preferred to wait for my guest or be seated. Well, that answered my question of whether Sammy had arrived or not. If this was business it would be considered rude to go ahead and take my seat, but not out of line. Sammy may have other ideas about what tonight was about, but as far as I was concerned, this was definitely a dinner date. And getting seated before Sammy got here would be bad form.

I had every intention of talking about everything and never once touching on anything about business. I wanted to drink wine, enjoy a good meal, and spend my evening with the beautiful Sammy Cole.

I couldn't find any information about her, other than what was publicly posted on Eyes On Care's website. I wanted to know everything about her from what made her smile, to what music she listened to when she was depressed. Was she a dark chocolate or a milk chocolate woman? Did she drink red wine or chardonnay in the tub?

I could get the numbers and information from Harper. I already forwarded the PowerPoint and spreadsheets to her for analysis. As far as I was concerned, Foundations Network Communications was going to partner with Eyes On Care. I really didn't care how it was going to happen, as long as it did. Anything to give me an excuse to have Sammy around.

I checked my Omega timepiece. I should have insisted on picking her up.

"It's not a date, Alex," she said when I suggested it. "You wouldn't pick up a male CEO, would you?"

"I might send a car." But she was right. I didn't pick up male colleagues. I didn't give a fuck about their personal lives. And good Lord, I did not want to know if any of them took bubble baths.

I was very eager to know if Sammy took bubble baths, or if she preferred to soak in hot water lightly scented with roses and honeysuckle.

I didn't like waiting near the entry, that made me look eager and put her in the position of power. I needed to maintain control of the evening, or she would have us discussing growth trajectory and ROI on advertising streams. Faced with the conflicting factors that this meeting was under the pretense of a business dinner, and the fact that I wanted to be a gentleman and escort my date to the table, I ground my back teeth together and sucked it up. I had no other choice but to wait.

Fortunately, she didn't keep me waiting long.

"Am I late?" she asked with insight.

"Not really," I said. In fact, she was exactly on time. I had been earlier than I needed to be.

"Shall we?" I nodded to the maître d' to take us to our seats.

Sammy was all grace and smiles. I walked behind and enjoyed the view as we followed to our table. I cleared my throat and adjusted my gaze as she took her seat.

"Have you been here before? I haven't. What should I order?" She didn't even look at the menu before asking me.

A waiter arrived and I ordered wine for us both.

She tilted her head and narrowed her eyes at me. "Wine? I thought this was not that social."

The waiter paused and gave me a questioning glance.

"I like wine with dinner. That doesn't make this any less official. Don't worry, I won't judge you for having a glass or two. No pressure."

Her laughter was sharp and cutting. "That feels exactly like pressure. I'll have sparkling water with lime for now."

The waiter left.

"What do you think you can learn over dinner that I wouldn't be willing to share in your office?" She was immediately on the defense.

This wasn't an attack or a campaign to get behind enemy lines. Clearly, she was on edge.

"Well, I don't think I would have discovered you prefer sparkling water over wine in my office."

Her face crinkled with a smile. Her nose lifted and her cheeks rounded. She was adorable. It was okay to think that because I left all business thoughts at the office. Tonight, was personal. Fully social.

"I didn't say I prefer it. But getting buzzed during any office function isn't smart, or classy."

I conceded. "You, madame, are definitely a class act."

So, my strategy was going to have to change. Tonight, was not going to end with her in my arms. I was going to have to play the long game with her. Something in my chest told me that was a smart thing to do.

"I now know that in addition to being an innovative thinker, you have a sense of decorum. Even more that I wouldn't necessarily have gleaned from across a boardroom table."

The waiter returned.

"Oh, geez, I haven't even looked. What do you recommend?" she asked the waiter.

I watched as they discussed a variety of cuts and preparations. When she engaged with a person, she was fully present. Maybe that's what had pulled me toward her. She was stunningly beautiful. I know that was my initial thought the first time I saw her. But that was a surface level assessment.

One awkward conversation, one inept action regarding her business could have easily changed my attraction to her. But every time I had to email her, talk to her over the phone, have a meeting with her, I wanted to know more, and be closer to her. Watching how she ordered her steak showed me how she treated people.

She paused, trying to decide between two different options.

"Why don't we get both," I said. "When they come out, you can decide which one looks the best to you, and I'll have the other one."

"Really? You would do that?" she asked.

"Why not. Everything sounds like it will taste great. This way I don't have to look at the menu and choose."

She turned her smile to the waiter. "I guess we'll have both then. And I'll have a red wine, whatever you suggest, something mid-range?" She looked at me and nodded.

"Sounds good to me," I said. "So, wine with dinner?"

"Wine with food more specifically."

I sat back and grinned. "See, I have already learned so much about you, and we've barely ordered."

"Fair point." She let out a light sigh and relaxed.

I knew my charm would win her over sooner than later.

"What do you want to know about me Alex?"

"How personal can I get?"

"I reserve the right to not answer you, and if you ask a single question about my underwear I'm out of here, and Foundation network Communications will not be welcome to continue a working relationship with Eyes on Care."

I sucked in a hiss through my teeth. "That sounds like it has happened before."

"It happens too often. Businessmen take one look at me, or Vanessa and they have a long list of assumptions that are completely off base, sexist, and straight up rude."

I took a drink of my wine. I knew exactly what she was talking about. I know I certainly had some unprofessional thoughts when we first met. At least I was smart enough to have kept my mouth shut.

"Tell me one of those assumptions, and how are they wrong."

She frowned and blew a huff of air between pursed lips. "Um, one of the biggies is that I didn't do the initial business model, that I stole the concept. Somehow, I am too young and too pretty to be thinking about child care."

I didn't say a thing. I nodded, encouraging her to continue.

"I started based on a very real need for affordable assistance so that I could attend classes."

"So that's your baby in the photos?" I adjusted my tie and sat up a little straighter. Had I made a rookie mistake of being attracted to a married woman?

She nodded. "That's my son. My mom had to suddenly move across the country to help her daughter and I was stuck in desperate need of help so I could go to classes."

"Wait, if she's your mom…"

"Oh, yeah, she's not my mother. I'm estranged from my birth family; Michelle was a mother by mutual choice. Actually, she was my boss. And when by surprise, I got pregnant, she's the one who helped me stay in school. And for your next question the father isn't in the picture." She paused and had a thoughtful look on her face. "He doesn't even know about Xan."

"Xan?" I asked.

She twisted and retrieved her phone. She held out a photo of a pale haired boy with large eyes and those tiny teeth toddlers had.

"That's my little man, Xander. I can't tell you how close Eyes On Care was going to be called Watch Xander. I'm not particularly good with names. Vanessa has a better marketing sense than I do."

Sammy's eyes sparkled as she spoke about her son.

"Let me guess, the next most annoying question is did your boyfriend do the program development for you?"

She smiled and began clapping her hands. "Women don't know how to code." She sighed again.

"Both Vanessa and I designed the first rendition of the platform we are still on. We did hire two very talented programmers who could spend all of their time focusing on ensuring that we functioned while Vanessa and I did all the other stuff that building a networking business model needs. And I don't have a boyfriend, so yeah, I did the work."

I was a little too pleased to get confirmation that she was single.

"You talk about Vanessa like she's a partner. I was under the impression Eyes On Care was a sole proprietorship with you being the only owner?" I asked.

Sammy nodded. "That's right. Vanessa didn't want the tax hassle of being a partial owner. She does earn a percentage above her standard salary, as do my two primary programmers. We've all been together since before we graduated college."

I spent the entire evening listening to her story. I could have listened to her all night long.

## 11

# SAMMY

He wouldn't stop smiling at me. It didn't matter if I was talking, or eating, or doing anything.

"I'm afraid I'm dominating the conversation." I took a sip of my wine and a bite of my steak. It was exceptional.

He tipped his glass in my direction before taking a drink. "I did ask."

He had. Now I was stuck wondering if he had asked to catch me in a lie, or to see if and how I mentioned that we were married.

"Are you going to tell me about you?"

"I'm afraid there is more about my private life available on the internet than I care for."

"Are you telling me you'd rather I look you up? What if I fall down a rabbit hole of scandal and intrigue?"

He leaned back in his chair and his grin grew wider. "I promise you it's all true. The secret marriage,"—

This was it, my gut clenched. I froze. Alex was going to stand up and announce that he had known me by a different name, that he paid me to be his absentee wife for business reasons, and that I was worse than a gold-digger. I didn't even pretend to like him for regular monthly payments.

— "the race cars, getting arrested in Dubai for nefarious deeds involving a sheikh's daughter, the secret lair made of crystals and waterfalls. I admit to all of it."

"Now you're just mocking me," I said in exasperation.

He made a face and started to laugh. "I did get arrested in Dubai. I promise no young women were dishonored."

"And the crystal evil genius lair?"

"I have a really big amethyst geode when you first walk into my house."

I caught myself staring at his lips again. I licked my own. "I like amethysts. Purple is a good color."

"Is it now? You don't wear a lot of color."

I lifted my finger and wagged it at him. "Too personal for a business discussion. I'm not answering that."

"Hey, I admitted to being arrested in a foreign country."

"That's on you. After all, you told me that I should trust my research on you and your business to the internet. It's almost as if you don't run a company that relies on online networking and implementing authentication systems."

He took a deep breath, his broad chest lifted, straining the buttons over his pecs. I was ogling him entirely too much for business. If anyone here needed scolding, it was me.

"Busted. I am enjoying this dinner with you, Sammy."

"Thank you. I'm having a very pleasant time too."

"Are you just saying that to coddle me, or are you really having a good time?"

I paused mid bite and shook my head. He watched as I finished my bite. I bit my lip and contemplated my next move. This was no longer a dinner meeting, to get to know more about the potential colleague. This was a competition. Time to volley this back to him.

"You mistake me for someone who has acting skills. I don't play games Alex."

He leaned forward on his elbows. "Not even a little chess?"

"I'm a programmer, I love chess. Let me guess, dinner was simply an opening move. You wanted to see how I would react. Pawn for pawn, right?"

"You're very perceptive Sammy."

"Then how about you just tell me what you want." I was more than ready for him to get it over with. His ego might be bruised, but neither of us had done anything that should upset him too much. Yes, I changed my name. At least now he got it right.

"I want to know your favorite color, Sammy."

"You want to blur the lines between business and getting too personal?" I asked.

He shrugged. "I'm good with clearly defined areas. Business"— he defined a boxed space with his hands, and then moved that box to the left— "and personal. Why can't we have both? Can you keep your work life and your personal life separate?"

I laughed. "I created a business solely based on my personal life. I'm a single mother who needs childcare. I can't say from experience if that's even a possibility."

Alex tilted his head to the side, made a little shrug motion with his shoulders and then looked at me. At first, I didn't know if he expected me to keep talking, or if he was trying to read my mind, or see through me.

I decided to look back. If there was nothing to say, then who was I to ruin the moment. Alex's face relaxed. His brow eased. The smile lines at the corners of his eyes faded as his grin relaxed, and then came back as his smile changed. He was seriously handsome.

I took this moment to look for Xander in his face. I saw it in the curve of his nose, the shape of his chin. Xander had his father's strong square forehead. Xander would develop the same worried line pattern than hinted across Alex's forehead. Xander's eyes were a similar color, only a little paler.

It was strange to see Alex in such detail. I don't think I ever had a chance to simply admire him this way before. Not even on our ill-fated honeymoon. And photos, no matter how many I looked out, certainly did not do this man justice.

This wasn't some kind of show down. I think we both realized it. Neither of us moved, not willing to break the perfect moment in time.

"Enjoying everything? Can I get you more wine? Dessert?"

The magic was broken. I gazed up at our waiter. "Tell me about your desserts."

He ran through what sounded like standard restaurant desserts, chocolate lava cake, a brownie with ice cream, and cheesecake. Nothing appealed to me at the moment.

I shook my head. "I think I'll pass." I also said no when coffee was offered.

"Are you so eager to get out of my company?" Alex's voice rolled like thunder.

"I think you know that's not the case. I have a sitter I need to get back to, and a little boy to put to bed. He is notorious for not cooperating at bedtime for sitters."

Alex nodded. I doubted he understood.

"I want to see you again, Sammy."

I smiled and suddenly couldn't meet his eyes. I nodded. "I'd like that. I think I could separate business and personal life."

I couldn't believe I was agreeing to go on a date with him. It was a little messed up, he was married, but he didn't know that I knew. Of course, he was married to me, and I was pretty sure he didn't know that.

"Friday night? This time I will pick you up."

"I look forward to it. Good night, Alex." I don't know where I got the strength to get up and leave, but I did.

When I got home Xander was asleep, and I made arrangements with the sitter, Dana, for Friday night. The next few days at work, I felt positively giddy. I did not tell Vanessa that I was going out with Alex. I should probably ask him what the protocol would be for us. We weren't competitors, but we weren't in alliance exactly yet either.

This time I dressed more casually for our date. It wasn't a business meeting, so I wore something a little more fun. Alex said he wanted to know my favorite, so I made sure to wear a purple shirt. The doorbell rang, and I was suddenly nervous.

Xander ran toward the door with a squeal. He loved answering the door and was always excited to see who was on the other side.

I scooped him up.

"Sorry Miss Sammy, he escaped," Dana said.

"Not a problem. Shall we see who it is?"

I opened the door to see a smiling Alex. I stepped back, silently inviting him inside.

"Alex, this is my son, Xander." I swallowed hard. It had been right on the tip of my tongue to say our son. But that was a conversation for another time.

Xander squirmed and I set him down. Alex watched him run off.

"I wasn't certain how dressed up I needed to be; I hope this is okay." I gestured at my clothes. I had a purple tunic with decorations and rhinestones at one shoulder over tight jeans and sandals.

Alex let his gaze drift over me. "You look great."

I bit my lip and followed him out to his car. I admired the way his jeans hugged his ass and thighs. The man still had the same physique of a Greek God when we got married. It was a sure bet that he still had that six pack of abs I remembered from six years ago. His car was large and black.

"I thought billionaire playboys drove hot Italian sports cars, not SUVs." I teased as I climbed into the passenger seat.

I had to wait until he climbed into the driver's side before he answered. "I do have sports cars. If you'd rather we can go back to my place and switch out cars."

I shook my head. "I guess I just expected something with more show. Maybe heading back to your place on our first date might not be a good idea."

"Don't brush off that idea so quickly. We don't know how tonight will end."

I had gotten pregnant our first time together. I wasn't prepared to repeat something like that. "I have a kid at home. I don't think tonight will end at your place. Besides, don't you have people you would need to warn or something?"

"No one. I'm on my own. I used to have a live-in personal assistant, butler, batman type. But he got married and moved to Canada. I haven't found anyone to replace him, so I am on my own as for now. Everyone else comes in during the day, so that's not a worry."

I let out a breath. I was concerned that Alex's assistant would recognize me. After all, he had hired me and gotten my wedding dress. It was good to know that Red was doing well. It was better to know I wouldn't run into him and have him reveal who I was.

# 12

## ALEX

Sammy's body was warm and somehow familiar in my arms. Kissing her was like nothing I had ever experienced before while at the same time it felt like I had been kissing her forever. Our lips twisted and danced and merged.

I buried my fingers into her mass of hair, holding her to me. Not that she needed to be kept in place, she was wrapped pretty firmly around me, and I pressed her back against the side of my SUV.

She pulled back with a heavy sigh. Her fingers trailed down my torso and hooked into my belt.

"I can't invite you in."

I growled deep in my throat. I wasn't in a good place to vocalize my disappointment. As much as I hated it, I understood.

I pulled her hand away. She was playing dangerously close to my cock. Her lower lip pushed out and pouted. I claimed that lip between mine, still holding her hand in mine.

"You had better go in," I managed to say.

She hesitated, keeping her body pressed to mine. And then she took a step back. I placed my hands on her upper arms and pushed her back another step. I held her arms for a second longer than necessary. The war in my brain raged between doing what was necessary or following my hormones. I managed to let go and pull my hands away from her.

"Maybe next time we can plan for more time?" My throat felt dry, my words desperate.

She bit her lower lip and nodded.

I stayed in place as if I was bolted to the ground and watched her turn and walk inside her house. Her hips swayed in a very beckoning motion. Every step of hers was an invitation to touch her body. My cock throbbed, responding to the siren call of her movements.

I clenched my teeth and breathed heavily through my nose. It wasn't until she gave me a little wave and her front door closed with her on the other side that I allowed myself to move.

I climbed into the driver's side and gripped the steering wheel until my knuckles turned white.

My phone buzzed. I glanced at it before clipping it into the dash mount. An involuntary smile took over my face.

"I had a lovely time. How soon before you ask me out again?" Sammy texted.

I hit the dial button. "I haven't even started the car yet," I mock protested.

"Well, I have Dana here and wanted to get on her schedule. She books up fast."

"Oh yeah? Is she one of your Eyes On Care success stories?"

"As a matter of fact, she is. Now, when should I schedule her for?"

I couldn't help but laugh. Sammy was so mild-mannered when dealing with her business, but tonight I was getting yet another glimpse of how and why she was so successful.

"When's her next opening?"

I heard them conferring before Sammy's voice returned. "She's good for Sunday. But I can't. Sunday is all booked up and Monday mornings are hard enough as it is. How about Monday night?"

I didn't need to look at my calendar to know that Monday night was out. "Have a Board meeting on Monday. How about Tuesday or Wednesday?" I really didn't want to wait a full week, and only see her on weekends. She stirred something in my chest, she had my hormones on overdrive. I wanted to see her sooner than later.

"Wednesday is good," Sammy announced.

My cock surged in my pants. I guess I was happier to hear her confirm than I realized. I shifted in my seat adjusting things back into place as we made arrangements for time, and if we should meet or if I should pick her up.

Since we would both be downtown, we decided that meeting would be best. Even if it meant that I wouldn't be driving her home, and making out in her driveway, I was still eager to see her again. Once our date was scheduled and everything planned, I reluctantly ended the call.

I stared at her front door for a long minute before I started the car and headed home. My phone buzzed. I glanced at it. Another text from Sammy. I knew she received the autoresponder that I was driving, the next text admitted as much.

By the time I got home, there was a long dialog worth of messages from her. The last one requested that I please text her back once I got home safely. I typed out that I was home and off to take a cold shower. She responded with "blush."

Time over the weekend dragged out. I avoided calls from my mother and Roy. They wanted to talk shop; well they could do that Monday evening at the board meeting. I caught myself hoping to see an incoming call or text from Sammy.

Sunday was much the same as Saturday with me trying to find something to keep my mind from wandering all over Sammy's curves. The spreadsheets of hers that I thought about had nothing to do with business and everything to do with my bed.

I rolled into the office early. The monthly board meetings always required extra prep work on top of my regularly scheduled activities.

"Hey boss," Harper chimed as soon as I strode past the assistant's desk on my way in.

"Oh good, you're here today," I said.

"It's a meeting day, of course I'm here. And it's a good thing. Roy has already called in twice." She held out a sticky note with a message scribbled on it.

I glanced at it and shook my head. "He's trying to get something out of me, as if I have insider trading information on our own company."

"You kind of do, seeing how you run things."

"I know, but for some reason, Roy thinks he needs that information before the rest of the board. He needs to let it go already."

Harper didn't exactly chuckle. "I started a pot of coffee in there for you. I'm pulling the monthly financials and department status reports as usual."

When Red left me, I tried to hire Harper away from Foundation Network Communications to work privately for me. She refused and claimed she much preferred the challenge of working for the company. She would get bored having to book my vacations and pick up my dry cleaning. I couldn't convince her there was much more to the role than that.

She was good at what she did. I made sure she knew how appreciated her work was and paid her better than her worth. The last thing I wanted was to try to find a new assistant at work when I was without one in my personal life.

"Thanks." I pushed into my office and shrugged out of my suit jacket. It was a sleeve rolled up kind of work day, no use pretending.

"Call Roy," I said to the smart device in my office.

"I've been waiting for you to call me back all weekend." Those were the first words out of his mouth.

"Roy—"

"Don't speak to me with that tone Alexander."

It was a good thing the man couldn't see my expression. Normally I would claim that eye rolls were the reaction of teenage girls, yet there I was rolling my eyes hearing my uncle's voice. I wasn't some kid to be scolded. I had a business to run and a meeting to prepare for.

"I need to know where we stand on this acquisition action item."

I let out a long, slow breath. "All of that information is being pulled together from my teams and will be presented tonight."

"I don't understand why you don't have this information at your fingertips. When I was in your office, I could pull these figures together in a matter of minutes."

I let him ramble on about how he was so much better suited for the CEO position than me. He completely disregarded the actual figures. Year after year, under my guidance, Foundation Network Communications increased revenue. We expanded our market base into different regions, and we had a notable increase in employee retention. In short, when I was allowed to do the job my father had raised me to do, we flourished.

Sure, Roy would have all of the acquisition information at his fingertips. He was a control freak and would have been the one to single handily head up those ventures. I preferred to let others handle the minutiae of the day to day.

I was being honest with myself here, the only reason I was hands on with the agreement development with Eyes On Care was Sammy. And, if I was being honest with my colleagues, I should let someone else take over those negotiations. I didn't know if I was capable of doing that.

"Unfortunately, Roy, I do not have that information at my fingertips. My teams are pulling together their reports. Have you remembered to RSVP for the dinner? We want to make sure catering has accurate counts. Are you down for the steak or are you still thinking about listening to your doctor about your cholesterol. I can get a message over to catering to switch you over to the salmon."

"I don't know what games you think you're playing," he got all blustery and tried not to curse at me.

"Roy," I cut his tirade off. "The figures will be presented this evening at the meeting. That's the end of it. There is no reason for you to have the information ten hours before anyone else. I am not trying to pull a fast one. Now, I have a long day ahead of me. I have an acquisition to assess on top of getting the monthly report pulled together for tonight's meeting. Please stop harassing my assistant."

That ended the calling for this month. He'd start the cycle again the week before our next board meeting.

# 13

## SAMMY

The podcast I was listening to was interrupted by a computer voice announcing I had a call. I hit the answer button on my steering wheel.

"This is Sammy," I said.

There was a moment of silence, and then a hacking cough. I waited while the coughing continued.

"You okay there?" I asked.

"I can't make it tonight," a thick groggy voice said.

"Dana?"

"Yeah, I'm sorry. Some kid has given me the plague. I feel like shit. I'm really sorry."

"These things happen." I sounded more understanding than I felt.

"I meant to call, but I've been asleep all day."

I felt guilty for my moment of unkind thoughts regarding Dana's illness. She sounded bad.

"I'm so sorry Sammy. I know you had a hot date planned."

"It's only a Wednesday, not that hot of a date. You rest and feel better. Do you need anything? Vitamin C, cough medicine, orange juice, soup?"

There was more coughing.

"My roommate went out and stocked up on all the meds. I'm good."

"Feel better and stay hydrated."

The call ended and I groaned. I pulled into the parking lot of Xander's daycare and made a quick call before I went in to pick him up.

"Sammy." Alex's voice gave me goose bumps and felt soothing all at the same time.

"Hey, Alex," I started.

"No," he dragged the word out. "Please do not tell me you are calling to cancel."

"What do you want to hear instead?" I giggled. He reduced me to blushes and smiles.

"Hm, something probably too risqué to say this early in our dating history. But it involves what you may or may not be wearing."

I giggled again. "Sorry to disappoint on all fronts. I think my skirt is Calvin Klein, it might be Ann Taylor, so business basics. Nothing racy, nothing lacy. And I have to reschedule. My sitter is sick."

He groaned. "This is where I comment on the irony of the founder of a sitters network platform unable to have childcare for a date."

"Yeah, it is. But at this short notice, it's not going to happen."

"I still really want to see you. Are you open to options?" he asked.

"What kind of options are you talking about? I can't bring Xander with me. He does have a bedtime routine I would like to stick with."

"If you can't bring Xander out on the date with you, could I bring the date to you and Xander?"

It took me a moment to figure out what he meant.

"You want to come over? I don't know Alex. I'm not exactly prepared to make a fancy dinner."

I heard the low growl again.

"Sammy," he let out a sigh. "I don't care if we eat McDonalds. I just really want to see your smile tonight. That sounds ridiculous, I know. You don't have to do anything. I'll pick up dinner on the way. You don't even have to clean anything; I just want to hang out with you." He paused. "That makes me sound desperate. The offer stands, but I understand if you can't tonight, we can reschedule. I didn't mean to get pushy."

I shook my head and bit my lip. He was giving me a way out. Silly man. I was ready to say yes.

"Can we have Italian? Xander likes spaghetti with meatballs, and breadsticks," I said in answer.

"Italian sounds great. Wine mid-week okay, or not with the kid?" he asked.

"I have some red, enough for a glass each," I said.

"Do you have a favorite, or should I surprise you?"

"I'm in a spaghetti or ravioli mood, I'll let you choose. But definitely bread sticks, lots of them."

He chuckled and said he would take care of picking up dinner and would see me at my place in about an hour.

I was glad our date didn't need to be rescheduled. I wanted to see him as much as he wanted to see me.

"Momee!" Xander ran and jumped at me.

I caught him in my arms and gave him a sloppy kiss on the cheek. "Hey, baby. Did you have a good day today?"

He nodded and started playing with the collar of my blouse.

I signed him out of the day care and carried him to the car.

"Do you remember when I said you would get to play with Dana this week?" I asked as I buckled him into his car seat.

"Let me." He took the buckles from my hands and pushed the clips together until they clicked.

I assisted on the last one. "Good job."

"Dana tonight?"

I shook my head. "Dana got sick. So, Mommy is staying home."

His little lower lip stuck out on a pout.

"But Mommy's friend is coming over. We'll have dinner, and watch a movie just like if Dana came over, okay?"

Xander didn't seem bothered by the change in plans after he learned we could still watch his favorite movie. He then proceeded to babble about his day and how Hunter and Liam got in trouble and had to do a time out, but he didn't have to because he shared.

The rest of the commute home went smoothly.

Once in the house, I changed into leggings and a comfortable tunic. Alex had said he didn't mind if I didn't clean anything, but I frantically cleaned the living room and guest bathroom. Everything I didn't have time to find a place for got dumped into a laundry basket and put in my room behind closed doors. I contemplated giving Xander a bath early, but with a spaghetti dinner, I ran the risk of having to wash him down a second time.

Nerves danced up and down my spine as the time got closer to when Alex was supposed to arrive. When the doorbell rang, it felt like I was going to jump out of my skin.

Xander dashed past me as he bolted for the door.

"Xander, what did I tell you?" I tried not to snarl, but that boy needed to learn not to open the door to anyone who rang the bell.

"Who are you?" he bellowed into the crack where the door met the frame.

"It's Alex. I'm your mom's friend. I have spaghetti and meatballs for you."

Xander flung the door open wide. My kid was definitely the one who would be lured into some strangers' van with the promise of candy.

"Hi," I managed as soon as I saw Alex.

He had a grocery bag in one arm, and another one sitting on the ground next to his feet. His suit looked rumpled from a long day. His tie was loosened and skewed to the side. His dark hair ruffled from having run his hands through it entirely too much.

He looked like he was coming home. I blinked a few times and hurried to get Xander out of the way so I could take the bag from Alex.

"I've got that," I said as I took the bag.

He picked up the other bag and stepped inside.

"This smell delicious," I said.

"The drive from the restaurant was so tempting. I wanted to reach in and grab the bread sticks."

"I can imagine. Thank you for getting dinner. Xander, will you get napkins on the table?" I tried to give him something to do so he wouldn't get under our feet.

Once in the kitchen, I set the bag down. Alex slid the bag he was carrying down and then leaned in and kissed me on the cheek.

"Thank you for having dinner with me tonight."

I tried not to blush. "Thank you for suggesting it. I had been looking forward to our date. I was a little upset when Dana called, but she sounded really sick."

Alex started to put the to-go containers from the bags and set them on the counter as I pulled out plates and handed forks to Xander to put on the table. The smell of warm tomato, garlic, and Italian seasonings had my mouth watering. I was more than ready to eat.

Having Alex at the table with us felt insanely familiar. Xander was quiet, the way he behaved around a new person until he felt more comfortable. He was also hungry and ate three breadsticks and a full plate of noodles.

I had ravioli in marinara sauce, a salad, and at least three breadsticks myself.

"What do you think they make these with?" Alex asked as he broke another breadstick in half and started to eat it.

I shrugged. "Crack. It's the only thing I can think of. They taste like bread, but they are addictive."

"Down," Xander started to squirm and get a little whiny.

"I don't understand whining, try again."

"I'm done. Down." He was getting tired. I helped him down and then handed him his bowl. He walked back into the kitchen and put it next to the sink.

"Good job," I told him. "Go pull out your PJs for tonight, I'll be right there." I turned back to Alex. "Keep eating or go watch TV. I need to give him a quick bath and get him in PJs. I promised we would watch his favorite movie before bed."

Alex glanced at his watch. "It's still early."

"Xander's bedtime is no later than eight thirty. And we have to fit in a bath and a movie."

"You do this every night?" Alex asked.

I nodded. "Yeah, that's what being a parent is. Every day, you get your little one to follow the routine. I know this isn't what you were expecting."

He reached out and cupped the side of my cheek, tilting my face so that I met his eyes. "It's not what I was expecting because I didn't know what to expect. I'm glad I'm here. You go bathe your son, and I'll put all of this away."

"You can leave it; I'll get it later."

"Not a problem." His soft grin made my insides melt.

# 14

## ALEX

S imply being around Sammy felt different than any other time I had dated a woman. So far, our dates were more about being in each other's company than being in each other's pants. But that wasn't the source of this feeling.

I cleared the table and repackaged the remaining portion of Xander's spaghetti and meatballs. I know Sammy said to leave it, but there was no way I was going to do that. She had a kid to manage, and she was fitting me into her life because I said I wanted to see her. Cleaning up dinner was the least I could do. After all I wasn't some brat, and she wasn't my maid. I was an adult man who knew how to take care of himself, and that included cleaning a kitchen— within reason.

I could do it a damn sight better than my father or my uncle could have. I don't think either of those men knew how to cook a meal. I had learned how to fish at their sides, and they could gut a fish and grill it, but I doubted they knew a thing about putting away dishes and washing up afterward.

I had been that guy too, in college. I had sucked, no clue how to do anything for myself. Mother either drove across the state to do my laundry or she paid for a cleaning service to come and take care of my dorm room and provide laundry service.

It took one girlfriend to ask me if I was an adult-man or a man-baby for me to realize that there was nothing to be proud about as a person who could not take care of my own basic needs. It didn't matter if I could afford to pay people to cook and clean for me— which I did— the fact that I couldn't do it became a matter of consciousness.

By the time Sammy and Xander returned in clean pajamas, ready for a movie before bed, the table where we ate dinner was cleaned off. Dishes were rinsed and stacked, and the leftovers were in the refrigerator.

"Alex, you didn't have to do all of that," Sammy said as soon as she and Xander came downstairs.

Her condo wasn't very big. A center unit in a row of townhouses, the main floor had a kitchen, a living room, and a dining area that was halfway between the kitchen and living room. From the look of it there was a backyard with a plastic play structure on it. I guessed that upstairs were the bedrooms.

"You let me come over. I felt as if I may have put you under pressure."

She stepped in close. She smelled of bath soap. Her hands caressed my chest. I snaked an arm around her waist to hold her in close. Her warmth pressed against me.

She lifted up on her toes and placed a quick kiss against my lips. "You are ridiculously attractive being all domestic."

"It's starting," Xander yelled.

Sammy stepped back and pulled me a few steps into the living room. Xander stood in the middle of the room, TV remote in hand. The studio's animated logo danced across the screen.

Sammy pulled me onto the couch next to her. And then Xander wiggled his way between us.

"Is this, okay?" she asked, catching my eyes.

I smiled and nodded. It was more than okay. A lump formed in my throat. Dating Sammy meant dating a family, and suddenly it's all I wanted.

The movie ended and Xander was limp with sleep.

"Don't go anywhere," she told me as she struggled to pick him up. "I swear he doubles in size once a week."

"Let me." I lifted the sleeping child into my arms. He weighed next to nothing. "Lead on."

I followed her upstairs, past a closed door. Was that her bedroom? Did she have a boudoir with mood lighting and lavish décor? I changed my mind about her room when I saw Xander's.

The kid's room was a Jurassic dream with dinosaur stuffed animals and large fronded potted plants. The walls were painted in shades of green and had large applique stickers of different dinosaurs. The bedding was even more dinosaurs. The funny thing was, Xander hadn't talked about them at all, and the movie, his favorite, was about fish and sharks.

I placed the sleeping boy in his bed. Sammy stepped up as I stepped back. She tucked him in and kissed his forehead. Something inside of me tightened, like a lock down on a dam of emotions. I understood envy.

I wanted what Sammy and Xander had. Complete trust, unconditional love.

I waited for her in the hall. When she stepped out of his room, I pulled her into me. Sliding my hand around the back of her neck, I held her to me as I took the kiss I had been longing for days. I poured energy and intent into my actions as our lips slid together, paused, pressed. My tongue danced out to taste hers.

She eagerly sucked me in. She pressed her body against me and tugged me close.

Her hands splayed across my back and then clenched, her fingernails pricking through the fabric and into my skin.

"You know what I really want right now?" I managed to say as the kiss paused.

She shook her head.

"I want to see your bedroom."

She laughed. The noise shocked her as much as it caught me off guard. She slammed her fingers over her mouth and dragged me back downstairs. I hadn't thought it was that bad of a suggestion.

"The only reason my house looks clean is I shoved everything into my bedroom. There is no way you are seeing that tonight."

Hands still together, I swept her around and back into my embrace. "Sounds like a future possibility though."

Sammy played with the buttons on my shirt. "Alex, I..."

I kissed her, stopping her words. The kiss wasn't long or deep, but enough to interrupt her. "Do not let me bully you or pressure you into anything you don't want. That goes for dating or the merger. I feel like you did that by letting me enter into this private evening between you and Xander."

"I'm glad you came. I wanted to see you, too. Dating is a lot different with a kid. I haven't been able to go out much. A lot of men instantly run when they find out kids are involved."

"I'm not one of those men."

"No, you aren't. So, you're okay with Xander being part of all of this, whatever this is?"

I kissed her again, this time because I wanted to reassure her. "I like you, and I like him. I understand you are a combo pack. If I was looking at this from a business perspective, I'd say it's a good investment of time and effort."

"Yikes, I don't know if I want to be considered an investment. But I think I know what you mean. And I would like for there to be a future possibility of you seeing my bedroom, but not tonight."

"Tell me, Sammy." I kissed her more, and this time I let my lips linger on hers. My body delighted in the softness of her and the way she seemed as hungry for me as I was for her.

Her bed was not an option, but her couch lured us into its depths. Her hands stilled mine when I reached for her waistband and tugged on hems. She looked deep into my eyes and then up at the ceiling. Right, we were not behind closed doors. I would have to be content with kisses and touching her through her clothes.

I didn't know what time it was when she pushed away from me with a groan. "Tomorrow starts too early for us to stay up all night making out."

"But it could be fun." I tried to tug her back against my chest.

She didn't budge. "Time to kick you out, Alex."

"You are a cruel woman Sammy," I teased. "Home alone to a cold shower."

Back on my feet, with my jacket and my tie hanging across my arm, she held my hand as she dragged me to the door.

"When can I see you again?" I asked. She was like some kind of a drug in my system, and I needed to know when I would get my next fix.

"You are welcome to come over on Friday," she said.

"Do you have enough time to find a sitter? Not that I doubt your platform, but it would be a great way to demonstrate the effectiveness of

Eyes On Care to the CEO of that other company you are in negotiations for a partnership with."

Sammy's eyebrows went up.

"Partnership? Oh, I do like the sound of that. So, Friday. Here if my platform lets me down?"

I wrapped both arms around her. I did not want to let go or leave. "Dinner and my place when it works. And I will make sure my place is clean, because I really want to show you, my bedroom."

She bit her lip and smiled. "Do you have a big dinosaur poster you want to show me?"

"I have something big I want to show you, but it's not a dinosaur poster. Plan to stay late, very late."

## 15

# SAMMY

"In a staggering display of Eyes On Care platform's effectiveness, I have secured a babysitter for Friday night," I texted Alex. This occurred on Thursday with slightly more than twenty-six hours' notice. Both the caregiver and the client are pleased with the transparency of going child care rates in the area, so that the negotiated fee reflects both the short term nature of the notice, as well as the after-hours time frame.

We were moving forward on defining exactly what the working relationship between Eyes On Care and Foundation Network Communications was going to be.

"This is fantastic news. But one question."

I waited for his next text.

"Is this information I should print out as a case study for my business files, or…???"

I shook my head, surprised he didn't throw in an emoji for good measure.

"I think you can safely include that in a case study if you wanted. But this is for you specifically. I got a babysitter; you have twenty-six hours' to get your room clean."

I bit my lip and giggled a little too maniacally.

"What's so funny here?" Vanessa asked as she popped her head into my office.

"I'm sending some stats to Alex. He's a bit of a flirt," I said. I wasn't exactly lying. The time in which I located a qualified sitter was pertinent to the growing business relationship. I just didn't need to share with her that I was teasing him about having clean sheets for our date.

Butterflies erupted in my stomach. Oh gods, I was flirting with the intent of sleeping with him. Reality slammed into me, and my nerves rioted.

"You, okay? Sammy, you've gone pale."

I shook my head and shuddered. I quelled the instant flood of panic. I wasn't like I hadn't slept with Alex before. Last time I walked away with Xander, only I hadn't known that for a few months. This time I wanted to walk away with Alex.

"Yeah, I'm fine. Just got a weird chill."

"Someone walking over your grave?" she asked.

"Exactly that kind of feeling. I was just sending some stats over."

"That's what you said. Do you think this deal is going to go anywhere?"

"Why? You found us a great prospect. These things take time, at least that's my understanding. And I know Alex seems motivated to make this work."

"You're awfully chummy with him," Vanessa said.

I had a split second in which to decide to tell her everything or keep what was going on between Alex and I strictly between us. I opened my mouth, thinking I was going to say I'd gone on a date with him, but that's not what came out.

"We've been emailing. He's not familiar with the needs of families that need to secure sitting services. I've been sharing some success stories."

"Sounds like we need to put together some case studies. Follow a few caregivers around," she suggested.

"Exactly and get the families point of view as well."

By the time Vanessa left my office we had a set of questions and opinion polls to go out to find our case study subjects. It was a good thing, because the next day I was in and out of meetings with our accountant and the annual financial auditor. No time to brainstorm case studies. No time to be nervous about my date with Alex.

Xander settled in with the new sitter, and I saw no reason to hang around my place. I arrived at Alex's doorstep five minutes early.

"I thought you would never get here," he teasingly scolded me before sweeping me into his arms and claiming my lips.

"You had something to show me?" I returned his kiss eagerly. I didn't care about dinner, or food. I wanted Alex as much as he wanted me. More so, because I knew who he was and what he was capable of. I had been in his arms before, and I hadn't touched another man since.

One or two dates to soothe the nerves of my friends who were concerned I wasn't dating was the maximum I had dipped my toe into the dating pool after I had Xander. I didn't have time; I didn't have interest. None of those dates had been my husband.

And now I was back in his arms. I knew our marriage was strictly for some legal status, and a financial pay-off, but I had fallen hard for Alex. Even though I knew I shouldn't have. And even though alarm bells were filling my head with their warning, I didn't care. Alex wanted me, it's all I ever dreamed about.

I sucked his tongue into my mouth when it darted from between his lips. He consumed me, as I tried to capture every lick, every nibble with my lips.

Alex walked backward, leading me into the depths of his home. I didn't pay any attention to any of it. My mouth was on his, my hands roamed over his arms, across his chest, down his back. I wanted him, all of him. I could get a tour later, after I could no longer think, and could barely walk because I knew he would leave me legless and limp.

And then we were falling to his bed. It was soft, but I didn't even notice or care if it was freshly made or not. All I cared about was the man in my arms, his touch, his skin.

I kicked out of my sandals and tugged at his belt. When his hand slipped under the hem of my tunic and caressed my skin, I let out a soft gasp. He pulled the top over my head, only breaking eye contact when the fabric obscured our view.

He watched me the entire time I undid the buttons on his dress shirt. And he kept his eyes locked with mine as I unfastened my bra. When he looked down at my exposed breasts, he let out a growl.

I felt like laughing triumphantly when he wrapped his hands around the sides on my breasts and buried his face into the softness of them. His thumbs stroked over my nipples sending electrical pulses straight to my core. I moaned and held him to me as he sucked and gently bit at my skin.

There was no struggle to divest ourselves of the rest of our clothes, and then we were skin to skin. Every last inch of Alex felt warm, smooth and just perfect. Even the way the hair on his legs tickled my skin was a sensation to luxuriate in.

"Are you even real?" I asked.

"Why do you say that?"

"I can't believe I'm in your room." My voice was a whisper.

"Alex, look at me. Look at you. Men like you aren't usually seen with someone with my figure."

"Those men are fools and missing out. I like your abundance of curves. I like the way you are soft and yield to my touch. You wouldn't be here if I didn't want you, and I want you more than I should."

His hand gripped onto my hip and rolled me until I was under his weight. He positioned himself between my thighs. His cock was hot and heavy as it brushed against my wet core. I don't know why I doubted he was attracted to me.

He had been inside me before, and his cock certainly wasn't being coy. It was thick and protruded from him proudly, ready to be admired, ready to be inside of me. I lifted my hips and slid my legs over his.

"Let me convince you." He ran the head of his cock around my clit.

My sensitive bundle of nerves reacted, sending electrical pulses through my pussy, and illuminating my body with desire.

"Oh, Alex." It was sublime torture as his cock ran over my folds.

And then it was pure magic as he slid into me. His cock stretched and filled me. I had forgotten the exact sensation, even though I had dreamed about Alex making love to me often. This was better than any dream. Better than any memory, though I treasured that memory more than any pirate loved gold.

And now... I gasped and moaned as he slid in and out of my body. Pushing us both to the precipice of ecstasy. Alex had a very smooth rhythm, it was my urgent need that demanded he go faster, harder. I thrust my hips to meet him at twice the rate he moved. It was a dance of the ages, of perfection.

Our orgasms crashed together simultaneously. I didn't want it to end, but my body was satiated. I purred like a happy cat as Alex wrapped me in his arms. Breathing heavily, comfortably wrapped around each other we slipped into a light sleep.

When I woke up, it was later than I had expected.

"I have to go," I whispered as I kissed him. I slid from the bed and pulled my clothes on. The soft fabric felt harsh and scratchy after his touch.

"Can't you stay? Your sitter isn't expecting you until late." Alex pulled on his shorts as I finished getting dressed.

I shook my head.

He followed me to the front door. Before I could open it, he grabbed my hand and pulled me back into his arms. Did he have any idea of the effect he had on me? I wanted to melt against him and stay until it was time to get up and pour cereal for breakfast.

"I can't stay the night."

"I know. It's not fair of me to ask. But next weekend, come to the lake with me. I'll teach Xander how to fish, or how to swim if it's warm enough. And we can have a sleepover every night. Take Monday off and we can make it a long weekend."

He ran his fingers down the side of my face and caressed the skin at the base of my neck.

"That sounds like a very nice idea."

# 16

## ALEX

"How is this supposed to fit in here?" I called from the back of the SUV. I had one knee braced on the car's seat and was fighting the tether. Sammy had said it would just hook in since my car was a current model. Xander's car seat wiggled around as if it wasn't secured at all.

She carried a tote bag out and set it in the open trunk space.

"Let me see," she said as she shooed me out of the way.

"Does he even need the car seat? He's five."

"Have you seen my son? He's a skinny little boy. He weighs next to nothing. He's nowhere close to recommended limits for upgrading to a booster seat or being out of a car seat."

She crawled into the back of the SUV and fixed the kid's car seat. I don't know what she did next, but she jumped out of the car with a satisfied look on her face. She reached back in and gave the kid's car seat a hard pull. It didn't move.

I reached in and tried. Stuck solid. There was an entire set of parenting skills I did not have. Of course, not being a parent yet, there wasn't a reason to. But dating a woman with a kid meant I needed to step up my game.

"Damn, you're hot," I said.

"Why? Because I know how to secure Xander's car seat?"

I reached out for Sammy, grazing my hand over her hip until I could grab onto her and pull her in close.

"Competency is sexy," I said in a low voice as I bundled her in even closer. I looked down into her face, at her plump lips. I closed my eyes and dipped down to claim her mouth when a skinny little boy slammed into the two of us with a great deal more velocity and impact than his weight should have allowed.

Change of plans. No longer kissing Sammy, I reached down and ruffled Xander's pale hair as he grabbed onto the two of us in a group hug.

"Are we going yet?" He asked. His eyes were large and pleading as he looked up at Sammy.

"I almost have everything in the car. Do you have Trikey?"

With a wail of concerned anguish, Xander let go and rushed back into the house.

"That's his stuffy," she explained.

"A triceratops?" I asked. "That's his favorite?"

Sammy bit her lips together. "If you remember that, he will adore you forever."

I winked as I let her go. Following Sammy into her condo, I tucked Xander's favorite dinosaur into my memory, right next his mom's favorite color, purple.

"Anything else?" I asked as I held my hands out for her bags.

"Purse, phone…" She looked around until Xander was in front of her. She put her hand on his head. "Kid. That's everything."

"All right, lake house here we come."

With a squeal of enthusiasm, Xander ran out the front door. I was close behind him as he climbed into the back seat. I put the last of Sammy's bags in the back and activated the tailgate close as she locked up her home.

I closed Xander's door and slid in behind the wheel. The car was running by the time Sammy buckled in and closed her door.

"Hey," Xander said as I started to back up. "What about me?"

"What about you?" I asked.

"I'm not buckled in."

I stopped the car and threw it into park. Sammy gave me a look that I interpreted to mean I was dumb. I deserved it.

"I thought he knew how to buckle himself in." I confessed as she clipped him into his car seat.

"Did you ask?" She was not happy with me; her disappointment was all over her tone.

I waited until she was back in the car and buckled in. I put my hand on her arm until she looked at me. "I'm learning. That was a mistake. I will do better."

She glanced back at Xander and blinked a few times before returning her gaze to meet mine. "He's all I've got, Alex."

My gut clenched as I realized she was trying hard not to cry. She wanted to trust me, and I had fucked up in the very first moments of our weekend. "I will do better. I swear."

I didn't put the car back into gear and start driving again until she nodded.

My place in the city was more of a show piece than luxury and comfort. The lake house was comfortable. Large space, overstuffed furniture, right on the lake with my own dock.

"When you said lake house, for some reason I thought you had a cabin, or something more modest," Sammy said as I pulled into the drive.

"Why go smaller when you can go bigger?"

She laughed. "That's the most Texan thing I've ever heard you say."

"Then you haven't been paying attention." I unlocked the door and set the alarm for home.

Xander raced inside and began running in circles through the living room.

"Hey, we don't run inside," Sammy said.

I took the bags from her and headed toward the stairs. "Come on, I'll show you your room."

The guest room was boring and white with a blue bedspread. I hadn't bothered decorating the rooms I didn't use, but Mother has insisted that I provide basic bedding in all of the bedrooms, just in case. I would have to remember to thank her for that.

"Ew, this is boring, there are no pictures," Xander complained.

"Don't be rude sweetie. This is a nice room. It's really big. Did you see the bed? You get this whole thing to yourself," Sammy said in soothing tones.

"Where's your room?"

She looked nervously at me and then returned her attention to her son. "Alex and I are going to have a sleepover. I mentioned that. Alex, why don't you show us your room, so Xander will know where to find me if he needs something."

That's the moment I realized I was going to need pajamas for the weekend.

"This way." I led them down the hall to my room. The walls were painted a dark blue, and there were pieces from a local artist hanging on the walls. There was a very stark difference between the rooms I lived in and the ones I didn't.

"Can I have a sleepover too? I want to sleep in the big bed with you," Xander sounded whiney.

Sammy lifted him into her arms and mouthed 'didn't sleep in the car,' at me.

"Why don't you lay down in here and take a little nap, but you'll sleep in the other room tonight, okay?"

He nodded, and suddenly he seemed so much younger and smaller than my mental picture of a five-year-old had been. I left them alone and headed back downstairs to unpack the supplies we brought with us. As I emptied bags, my mental shopping list kept growing longer.

With a young kid in the house, I was going to need to sleep in something. Shorts would work in a pinch, but I already needed to go out, might as well pick some up. I also didn't think I had a life vest small enough for him. After the near miss of almost driving off without Xander being buckled up, there was no way I would even suggest he be allowed out on the boat without a life vest.

"Sorry," Sammy began as she stepped into the kitchen. "I thought he would sleep in the car, but he didn't."

"Not a problem. I realized I need to do some shopping, and this would be a good time to go."

"Are you sure?" she asked.

"Of course, I am." I stepped into her and wrapped my arms around her where she stood. "Nuances of dating a single mother. I'm motivated to get this right. Why don't you relax, wander around, get familiar with the house. Or take a nap with Xander."

"I can do that."

Kissing her was definitely one of the joys in my life. She was warm and supple. If she liked the kiss, and she seemed to like all of them, she made this little humming sound that went straight to my cock. Yeah, I was motivated to get things right this weekend.

"Text me if you need anything," I said as I left.

Once in the car I went into action mode. "Call Harper," I told the system.

"Alex, it's the weekend, this had better be good," she said.

"I know, sorry. I need you to locate a child life vest, and then see if it's anywhere within drivable distance to my lake house."

"Why do you need a kid's life vest? And why right now?"

I groaned deep in my throat. It wasn't unheard of me to bring clients and big vendors up to the lake for a day on the boat. So, I wasn't giving anything away if I confessed I had Sammy and her son here.

"I invited Sammy and her son from Eyes On Care for an afternoon at the lake. Her son is a bigger toddler than a kid."

Harper laughed. "I'm going to need a better description than that. But I can help."

With prompts from Harper, I was able to let her know that Xander felt like he weighed around forty-five pounds and was just over three feet tall.

"I'll call you back." She ended the call.

I pulled into the lot for one of those big discount department stores. This place should have what I needed.

"Okay boss; looks like the Supercenter on highway sixty-seven has what you need," Harper said as soon as I answered her incoming call.

"I think I'm actually in that store right now."

"Then, I'll leave the shopping to your capable hands."

I felt slightly abandoned when the call ended. But I was in the right place to get all the things that I needed. I grabbed a shopping buggy and went directly to the sporting goods area to pick out a neon yellow life vest for Xander.

# 17

## SAMMY

lex leaned over Xander and helped him hold the pole. Xander quickly flicked it over their heads and out into the water with a giggle.

"That's it," Alex spoke softly, encouragingly.

When he came back from running his quick errand, I thought he had lost his mind. I was a little glad he had. It was sweet. Xander was still asleep in the large bed in the master bedroom. So, I helped to unpack the car.

"You went out and bought more stuff than we brought," I pointed out. "What is all of this?"

"I had to get Xander a life vest," Alex started. "And I realized with him in the house, I should have something to sleep in. Explaining why mommy was sleeping with a naked man seemed like a conversation to avoid this weekend."

"Oh, you're planning on being naked?" I teased.

"And then, well. He looked so disappointed in his room."

Alex liked to wrap his arms around me when he spoke. I liked it too, so I didn't complain at all as he held me and continued to give me excuse after excuse as to why he purchased a new, dinosaur themed bedspread, a coordinating lamp, and area rug. There were also three movie posters, because those were the only dinosaur posters he could find. And three play sets with dinosaurs and action figures.

"My kid is going to like you better than he likes me," I complained.

I wasn't mad at all. In fact, I had to fight not to cry. It was one of the single most adorable things Alex could have done. Even though I had the hots for the man in a big way, I honestly had not expected him to take to Xander as well as he had. Maybe there was some mysterious biological connection, and they knew they belonged together. Maybe not. Either way, Alex was going above and beyond my expectations when it came to including my son.

By the time Xander woke up he had a second dinosaur themed bedroom. Alex made him wait in the hall before opening the door to show off the quick attempt at redecorating.

"I want you and your mom to come up to the lake house with me a lot. I figured you'd like it better if the room you stayed in was like your kind of room. I know you like dinosaurs, this should be exactly what you like." Alex made a presentation by opening the door to Xander's room.

Xander squealed in delight as he ran inside. The walls were still white, but there were posters, and the bedding had fun dinosaur designs on it. It was no longer boring than a hotel room as it had been previously.

Xander launched himself into Alex's arms. As Alex swung Xander around and they laughed, I stepped into the hall to catch my breath. Both of my guys were right there and happy. And I was miserable because I clung to the knowledge that they belonged together, and yet, I couldn't say anything to either of them. No one could know.

Xander didn't want to put his new toys down. It took the blatant bribery of going out on Alex's boat to get Xander to comply and go downstairs for lunch.

Alex gave us a boat safety lesson as I made sandwiches. And then we all changed and headed out to the dock. The house was right on the water. There would be no sending Xander out into the yard to play unsupervised for a few minutes like I could do at home. Our yard was tiny and fenced in. Here there was no fence. The yard went straight into the water. There was no slope of a beach, and it was deep enough for a boat.

I was spinning the worry wheels in my head for no reason. The house was pretty big for Xander to play inside, and if he went outside, there was no reason either of us couldn't also be with him.

Xander started complaining about the life vest, but as soon as Alex said no vest no boat, Xander settled down. I was surprised at how large the boat was. Then again, the lake house was huge. Alex didn't seem to do anything small.

"Oh, I don't leave it parked here when I'm not here," he said when I had asked about it.

"There's a guy at the local marina who will pull the boat from storage and have it delivered," he continued.

I could practically hear the chiming of old-fashioned cash registers ringing up how much everything cost. A quick trip to the store for a few last-minute items, cha-ching. An expensive boat kept in dry-dock storage delivered to his home with a single phone call, cha-ching. Luxury lake house with dock, cha-ching, cha-ching.

Eyes On Care was successful, and I was making good money. But I was clearly not at the same level of good money that Alex was. I was not in a financial situation where I could afford to upgrade the home I had, let alone afford a second luxury vacation home, multiple cars, and boats.

For someone who was used to such a lavish lifestyle I was impressed at how at ease Alex had been in my condo, eating take-out food, and cleaning up later. He never once commented on how my entire home could fit into the living room of his lake house.

I knew Alex had money. I had known from the very beginning. After all, who hired someone to be their wife for legal reasons? Only someone who was in a place to pay to begin with.

My gut clenched. If he wanted to take Alex, I was not in a position to stop him. I couldn't afford the same quality of lawyer that Alex probably kept on retainer if it came to a fight. That was one reason to not tell Alex who Xander was.

I pushed all that negative thinking aside. I was on a boat. The weather was glorious. I was with Alex and Xander was giggling. I was having a nice time. I needed to feel like it.

After a good forty minutes or so, the fishing got old. Xander didn't catch anything, and he felt this was completely unfair. Alex pointed out that he didn't catch anything either, but that didn't change the mercurial temperament change that turned Xander from a happy child into a pouting one.

I held Xander on my lap as Alex drove the boat back. I could tell they were both frustrated. They were so much alike. When Alex hit the wake of another boat and we bounced in the water, Xander started giggling again.

"Do that again!" he demanded.

Alex started smiling too. He spun the boat around in the water so that we crossed more waves and wakes, most of which he made with his boat. With everyone in a better mood, we stayed out on the water another few hours, only heading home as the sun got close to the horizon.

"Do we have to go home?" Xander whined.

"Can't be out on the lake in the dark, I don't have running lights." Alex's explanation was as simple as it came. Fortunately, Xander didn't argue.

We were all tired after an afternoon out on the water. I helped Xander with a bath and put on clean pajamas before taking a shower. By dinner time, I was more than ready to eat and then curl up to watch a movie before bed.

I made macaroni and cheese and added a can of tuna and some green beans. It was easy and simple, something I had learned to make as a kid. Something I knew Xander would eat. Worried that Alex would comment on anything from my cooking choices to my cooking skills, I had a moment of panic when I served a portion into a bowl for Alex.

Did rich kids grow up eating tuna mac? Has he ever had macaroni and cheese from a box and tuna from a can? Alex only said thank you as I handed over the food. He took his and Xander's dishes into the den so we could eat dinner and watch a movie at the same time.

My day ended as I followed Alex as he carried Xander up to his room. Once Xander was all tucked in, I let Alex help me into his room, and into his bed.

I curled up against him as he slid in close to me.

"Thank you," I murmured.

I snuggled against Alex's chest. His voice rumbled against my ear.

"You're welcome. I'm not sure for what, but whatever it is, I'm willing to take care of it again."

"Today was really nice. You were so good to Xander. You're good to me too," I said.

"I like you, Sammy. Xander is a great kid, besides, I need him to like me if I want to keep seeing you. I'm not above a little bribery," he said.

I wiggled so that I could reach his lips. I kissed him. It wasn't much of a kiss, but it was enough. If all Alex had done was hold me for the rest of the night, I would have been content. But he deepened the kiss, and then his hands began touching my body, caressing my soft spots.

Was this what being married with kids was like? I was completely exhausted after a long day, yet somehow, I found the energy to show Alex exactly how much I liked him, and how wonderful he made me feel.

# 18

## ALEX

I shouldn't have been surprised to see Roy and my mom in my office. The weekend had been one for the memory books. One I never wanted to forget. For a brief moment I finally understood why men wanted families.

It had nothing to do with controlling the will of others, and everything to do with that warm fuzzy feeling that sat deep in the chest. I got that feeling when I helped Xander buckle his life vest on and when I held Sammy in my arms. It was a feeling I couldn't ever remember experiencing.

It was the polar opposite of what I felt when I stepped into my office and was immediately confronted by my mother and my uncle.

"What's taking so long on this merger?" Roy stood up. He set his coffee cup down with more force than was necessary causing a spill.

My mother cleaned up after him.

"You're just going to let her do that?" I pointed at the mess he made.

"She's got it," Roy blustered.

I had disrupted his tirade, but I wasn't finished. "You made the mess, not her."

"It's okay, Alexander. Your cleaning staff wouldn't get here in time to take care of it. There, all done."

"That's not the point, mom. He made the mess, not you."

"Why are you going on about who made the mess? It doesn't matter who made it. Your mother took care of it," Roy said.

"No, Roy, that is exactly the issue here. You make decisions, you leave messes, you demand action, and you don't take care of anything. You come in here like you run this company. Let me remind you that you are only on the board, and only hold twenty percent of the shares. This is my company, my decisions."

"Who do you think is going to come in here and clean up after you make the wrong decisions? Who cleans up your mess?" He got louder as he grew more irritated.

"Not you," I said between clenched teeth. "And not her." I pointed at my mother.

"Alex," Mother said in a calming tone.

"Why do you let him treat you like this? He's worse than dad ever was." I looked directly at her.

"Alex, he's family. He takes care of me," she said.

Did she not see how he was holding some kind of power over her? I closed my eyes and refused to think that there might be something more going on between them. I did not poke my nose into my mom's personal life. I didn't want to know.

The dynamic between them was codependent, and wrong. She didn't make decisions without him, and I rarely saw him without her in tow.

"You two have been at each other's throats for years now. Isn't it time you figured out how to work together?" She pointed out the tension that always arose when Roy showed up out of turn to question me on my business decisions.

I forced a smile and sat down.

"You're right," I started. Turning my attention to Roy, I repeated, "She's right."

"You're dragging your feet on that babysitting proposal. I want to know why," Roy demanded.

I stretched my fingers out, and then tightened them into fists until my knuckles turned white. When was the last time he had been involved in a friendly merger? Had there ever been any during his tenure as CEO?

"We are taking our time getting to know the other company. Neither of us is in a rush to get to the signing table. They want us to know we are getting a quality product. Think of it like dating." My mind immediately went to Sammy.

Dating Sammy was different from dating any other woman I had ever dated before. There had been no three or five dates before sex rules, no you pay this time, I pay next time games. She hadn't shown up at my front door wearing only a trench coat and stockings with garters, and then kept me up all night screwing my brains out.

Dating Sammy was slow. There was no rush. We spent time talking and living. Dating Sammy was being in her presence and accommodating a five-year-old who some days acted like he was a teenager, and on other days behaved like he was still a toddler.

When it was time to take whatever our relationship was to the next level, there would be no doubts in my mind. I wouldn't question if we were moving too fast or jumping into something without due consideration. Whatever that next step would be, it would happen when the time was right.

"There is no deadline driving the decision-making process here. I understand your eagerness, but that is all it is. We still have case studies being conducted that will need to be reviewed and analyzed. We are still working out where they will fit in best to our big picture growth plan." I tried to explain.

Roy continued to glower at me. "If that's how you view dating, no wonder you don't go out much."

"Roy!" Mother practically shouted. "He's still a married man."

My gut clenched, and my chest tightened. Why did she have to bring that up while I still had images of the beautiful Sammy floating behind my eyes. I did not want to be reminded that legally I had a commitment, and a wife.

"Are you insinuating that my son is not a faithful husband?"

"I have never met the girl, and neither have you."

"Nevertheless, he is still married. Aren't you, Alex?"

I closed my eyes and wished I had taken a different approach to this entire conversation. "Yes, I am still married. But that doesn't mean I have forgotten how to woo a competitor."

"That's where you're going all wrong, son," Roy started.

I gritted my teeth.

"Dating isn't a competition," he said.

I shook my head. "I'm not talking about dating anymore. Bad metaphor, wrong example. The point I was trying to make was that there is no reason to rush this through. You show up and demand me to move faster doesn't do anybody any good. All it does is make you frustrated with me because I'm not doing things the way you want."

Roy grumbled. "Sounds like these people are dragging their feet."

"No one is dragging, Roy."

"Have you considered forcing them to comply?"

"I can't push a hostile takeover, if that is what you are implying. There are four stakeholders, that's it. There isn't some backdoor short-stick funding that can be done."

"Make them an offer they can't refuse," he said.

"That's exactly what we are working for. You've got to understand, Roy, when we buy-out or merge, or however the final deal happens, we also need to take into account the people who created that company. There is nothing without them. So, we need to know if we are simply buying the tech or are we combining efforts so they can use our marketing, and our knowledge to help them to expand. There are nuances to this that I feel you are missing in your drive to see this happen."

I looked at him for a long moment, and then shifted my gaze to Mother. There was something about her expression. She was keeping something from me.

"Is there something you need to tell me?" I asked her. Was there something else that was making both of them more eager for this merger, and the resulting growth in Foundation Network Communications?

"Mom, you aren't sick, are you?" I asked.

She shook her head.

"You aren't strapped for cash? Is everything fine with the house?" I asked more questions.

"What are you trying to get at, Alex?" Roy snapped.

"I'm trying to figure out what's in your craw about this merger. Why are you so eager to have it go through?"

"What's that to do with you, Mom?"

I shrugged. "I don't know, that's why I'm asking questions. Do you suddenly need an influx of cash? Do you need to liquidate some assets in a hurry, and wouldn't it be nice if your shares were worth a bit more than they are right now?"

"Neither of us is strapped for cash. I resent this line of questioning," Roy huffed.

"And I resent you pushing your way into my business, figuratively and literally, and trying to tell me how to run this place. I think we have come to a stalemate for the week, time for you to leave."

I stood up and walked to my office door. I was tired of this game that we played every few weeks. It left me with a bitter taste in my mouth at least through lunch. But this was my company, my birthright, and I was going to fight for it every single time.

Mother stood first. "You will still come to the Wine Tasting Auction on Saturday, won't you?"

"Yes, mom. I will be at your fundraiser."

Roy stormed past us. Mom looked at his retreating back, worried.

"Is there something I should be aware of?" I asked her.

"He wants to be useful," she said with a sad smile.

"Arguing with me is not useful. Find him a hobby, something other than harassing me about how to run this company."

"He's afraid of being obsolete, Alex. He likes to keep his mind active."

"He can do crossword puzzles," I complained. "Look, take him on a cruise. Do one of those river boats and go look at old castles in England or something. I will pay for it. I'm serious. One of these days our arguments are not going to end with hurt feelings and bruised egos."

# 19

## SAMMY

How was I supposed to return to my normal life in my small condo after a long weekend of luxurious living with Alex? He never once complained about the simple food I made, nor did he brag or say anything to make me think he was showing off when he took us out to dinner at the ridiculously expensive yacht club.

He went along with how we did things, and we did the same with him. It was amazing. It was dangerous. He still didn't know who I was to him, and yet he was already everything to me. I had fallen for him when we first got married. Those emotions and feelings were only cemented in place and reinforced the more time I spent with him.

The world felt like a let-down when I woke up in my bedroom, alone in my small home. I tried not to be gloomy for Xander's sake. But there were times he knew that mommy didn't feel happy. Suddenly being without Alex, I was cast low.

'Miss you,' I texted.

I tried not to be upset when he didn't immediately respond. He had a company to run. Hell, so did I, and I was well into my day before I heard from him.

Vanessa stood at my office door when the front desk buzzed my phone.

"Yeah?" I spoke.

"Alex Stone is on line three for you."

Vanessa's brows arched perfectly over her glasses. She didn't move, wanting to hear what he had to say. Instead of hitting the speaker I picked up the receiver. I didn't know if this was business or personal, and I didn't need Vanessa to find out I was sleeping with Alex this way. It was something I should tell her.

"Hi Alex, how are you today?" I said brightly.

"This morning has sucked. I had to deal with Roy and Mother, and I didn't see your text until later. I should have texted earlier," he said.

This was a personal call. I tried to shoo Vanessa away. She shook her head and made faces at me. I shook my head and waved my hand again. With an eye roll she pushed off the door jamb and reluctantly left.

"Sorry to hear that. My office has ears," I said.

"Then I'll keep this simple. I'd like to invite you, the CEO of Eyes On Care, to a charity auction on Saturday. Get a sitter."

"How do you know I'll say yes?" I teased.

"When have you ever been able to say no to me?" He had no idea how accurate that was. "It's black-tie, I'll pick you up at six."

My personal phone pinged with an incoming text as the call on the business line ended.

'I missed you this morning. We're going to have to do something about that.'

After reading his text, my mood went from standard Monday morning gloom to sunshine and daisies. It lasted until I realized that I had to get ready for a black-tie event. And then my mood immediately went into panic mode.

With the looming deadline of the charity auction the rest of the week seemed to speed by. I barely had time to find an appropriate dress, confirm with Dana for Saturday, and contract with her for an overnight.

"You look gorgeous," Dana said after I came out of my room.

There was nothing fancy or special about my dress. It was form fitted through the hips and then it flared out. It was designed to be a basic column dress but I was anything but column shaped so it hugged the curves I didn't mind showing off and was full through the areas that did not need to be emphasized. I kept my makeup simple but added a bit more color than normal to my lip.

She and Xander had a fun evening of pizza and video games and movies all planned. I had a long night of feeling out of my depth before I could be alone with Alex ahead of me.

The doorbell rang, and I let Dana run herd on Xander as he launched himself at the front door. He had it open and was tackling Alex before either of us could stop him.

"Hey, buddy. Did you answer the door without your mom again?" Alex asked as he stepped in with my son in his arms.

My heart lurched. Alex was insanely handsome in a tuxedo. He wore basic black, but he had a purple tie and pocket square. We definitely looked coordinated.

He put Xander down and reached out for my hand. "Beautiful, can I kiss you or will that ruin your makeup?"

"You can kiss me," I said.

His lips were warm, reminding me just how much I had missed him this past week. "How did you know to get a purple tie?" I asked.

"Educated guess. Your favorite color is purple. Odds are in my favor that you would wear a black or purple dress to a formal event. I could have been wrong, and you could have shown up in red."

I shook my head. "No red for me."

I made the last-minute information check in with Dana, hugged and kissed Xander goodnight, and then Alex whisked me off to the kind of party I thought only ever existed in the movies. There was a red carpet and local celebrities.

The organizers had turned the front lobby of the Children's Museum into a ballroom, complete with orchestra. It seemed like a lot of expense for a party that's primary purpose was to raise money. Around the edges of the dance floor where couples waltzed were tables lined with wine glasses.

"I thought this was an auction. This looks more like a fancy ball," I said as I leaned into Alex's arm.

"It's a bit of both, and more. At some point there will be an exposition dance, and then if you want to dance, you have to pay for floor time."

"That's an interesting way to raise funds. Get everyone interested and then charge them for it." The amount of money tonight would raise was simply staggering to think about.

"It's a sales technique. Those tables are for the wine tasting, and if you like what you taste you can then bid on individual bottles or cases. And"— he twisted around before directing me to our left— "over there is the silent auction."

I couldn't see what was being offered but it was safe to bet they were all high-ticket items.

"So, no penny auctions, huh?" I teased, mostly. Getting ready for tonight, the new dress, new shoes, and the cost of babysitting, financially put me out of the running on being able to participate in any kind of donation this evening.

Since I was here in the capacity of CEO of Eyes On Care, I did make arrangements to have a reasonable spending limit. Officially the company would make a donation, I just felt that it was going to be judged as small compared to everything else.

My stomach gurgled, and I felt a sudden sense of gloom take over. My hormones must have been out of whack. I had pre-period emotional dull drums that I typically got, only my schedule had been a bit off due to stress. My body had done this to me before, but not since that last round of final exams before graduation a couple of years ago.

"Alex!" A large voice boomed.

Alex's hands tightened on my back as we turned to face the voice. "My uncle," he said under his breath.

"Do I have to play nice?" I asked.

"Not if you don't want to." Alex raised his voice and introduced us. "Uncle Roy, may I introduce you to Sammy Cole. Sammy is the founder of Eyes On Care."

I extended my hand. I'd be as polite as Roy was. Not that Alex talked about his uncle, but he always seemed to be involved on the days Alex complained about busy bodies and work politics being a pain in the ass.

"That the company you're dragging your heels over?" Uncle Roy's eyes roamed over my body like I was a prize racehorse. "I think I understand why you're taking so long."

"Excuse me?" I spoke. I did not appreciate the implication. "I wasn't aware that there were any time issues regarding the current status of negotiations between our companies."

"There aren't," Alex practically growled. So, this was a sensitive point for him. I'd ask about it later. But if either of these two men thought I'd play meek to Uncle Roy's overt misogyny, they were wrong. "Roy is impatient to see us work out a deal."

I smiled. "I think we all want the companies to come together successfully. No need to rush things," I smiled as if I was enjoying myself. I really wanted to get away from his uncle. The man leered at me and made me feel uncomfortable.

"Ah, Mother. I was just about to set off in search of you." Alex had found an escape route faster than I had.

He went through the introductions again, and this time I felt the nerves in my stomach dance. This was my mother-in-law. No one but me knew it, but it still made me nervous to meet her.

"Excuse us for a moment, dear," his mother said after an exchange of a few pleasantries.

I nodded and meandered over to a table with wine. The table server explained how the tasting worked. I could buy a glass for the evening and sample the variety of vineyards and styles that were represented at the event, or I could purchase individual tastings.

I opened my clutch and pulled out a five. It looked like I would be limited to how much wine I would be drinking; I didn't carry around the necessary amount of cash to purchase a glass for the evening. But with five I could get a generous taste of the Merlot this table featured.

With glass in hand, I wandered back toward Alex and his mother and uncle. I really wish I hadn't. That gut feeling about not liking Roy had been justified. I overheard his vile opinion, and then Alex's mother agreed.

I left the wine I had barely taken a sip of on a tray with other glasses and ran for the entrance. I needed to get out of there.

## 20

---

# ALEX

"I can't believe you are here flaunting that woman," Mother said.

Roy said something, but I had already stopped listening to him. He treated Sammy as if she were a commodity on the market and not a potential business partner. And now, the more my mom said the less I paid attention to her words.

"You are a married man, and that woman is not your wife. You are out here flaunting your mistress. I can't believe you brought her to my event. These people are my friends. I'm going to have to explain who she was. What am I supposed to say when people think she is my daughter-in-law because you had your arm around her? If she is simply a business acquaintance, why does your tie match her dress? You should be ashamed. I'm embarrassed."

She went on and on. I didn't hear the words. I heard the pounding rush of blood through my veins and the droning noise of her infinite disappointment. My anger kept building with each resentful word either of them said.

"That woman you are being so rude about is my guest, and the CEO of a company we are trying to acquire. I suggest—"

"You suggest?" Mom cut me off. "Alex, you are in no position to suggest anything. Your wife would be the appropriate person for you to accompany to an event such as this. Your wife. Or is she even real?"

My gaze narrowed as my anger grew.

"Is she aware of your philandering ways? Are you so embarrassed by her? I told you, you should have married a slender woman, someone who would have kept her figure. Are you so embarrassed to bring her along? Does she know you see other women and now she won't be seen with you? Why is she in hiding, Alex?"

Mom kept barraging me with questions. I don't think she bothered to stop and breathe before she unleashed another question, I wasn't willing to answer. I turned and left. I wasn't going to give my mom any further opportunity to berate me about Sammy this evening. We would leave as soon as she was ready. I didn't want to stay any longer than was necessary.

I didn't see her. Where the hell had she gone? I scanned the crowd, still nothing. I stopped at the nearest tasting table.

"Did you see that woman I was with early? Shapely in a purple dress?"

The server at the table stared at me for a moment. I couldn't tell if they were thinking or if their brain had stopped working. "Yeah, she bought a taste and then just left it," they finally answered.

"Did you see where she went?" I asked.

They pointed vaguely toward the front of the event. "I think she went that way. Sorry, man, I was helping other people. I only really paid attention because I had spent some time going over how the wine tasting worked, and then she didn't even bother to try it after I poured her a full glass."

I thanked him and hurried to find Sammy. The crowd grew thicker around the doors as they came in and milled about before truly entering the event. I thought I saw her through the front windows.

Pushing my way closer, I saw that it was her. She rubbed her hands over her arms. It wasn't cold out, but she looked chilled and uncomfortable.

It was like swimming upstream through people trying to get through the entry doors and outside to her.

"Hey, what are you doing outside? Are you okay?"

She turned and blinked those big eyes of hers at me. She had been crying. I folded her into my arms and crushed her against my chest.

"Can you take me home? I'm not feeling very well," she said against my chest.

"Sure, I can."

We walked slowly to the valet stand where I requested for my car. I held her for the few minutes it took them to return with the car. Screw anything Mother had to say. I didn't care if anyone saw me holding Sammy. We matched because I wanted people to know I had staked a claim. Sammy was with me.

The car pulled up and I helped her into her seat.

"Do you need me to stop and get you any medicine?" My gut clenched with worry. I had never seen Sammy look so pale and sad.

"I just want to go home," she said in a small voice.

I tossed a couple of twenties at the valet and slid in behind the wheel.

Instinctually I began taking her to my home, because she belonged with me. I would take care of her. Before I turned left, it occurred to me that she would want her own home, her bed, her things.

I was still going to take care of her, she was mine. A surge of resentment twisted in my gut. My mother was right, I had a wife. Some woman named Abigail who I could barely remember. The resentment in my gut roiled.

I resented my past self for having taken such callous action. I got married. It seemed like a good idea at the time. It had served a purpose at the time. But I had to get drunk to make it through the day. Mistakes had been made. Checks had been cashed.

I now had control of my business, and Abigail had been all but forgotten.

The initial agreement had been for five years. Our sixth anniversary was approaching. I only knew this because I celebrated finally having Foundation Network Communications. Now that was a date worth remembering.

I glanced over at Sammy. She rested quietly, looking out of her window. I reached over and squeezed her knee. "Are you doing, okay?"

She rolled her head across the seat back to face me. She looked sad. I wanted to pull the car over and pull her into my arms and hold her until she smiled.

"I'm sorry, Alex. I know you were looking forward to having a good time. It came over me so suddenly. I don't even think I managed to taste the wine sample before I felt nauseated. I thought fresh air would make me feel better, but it just made everything worse."

I gripped the steering wheel. "Don't worry about it. I'll get you home soon."

I was looking forward to an evening with her. It didn't matter to me if we were dressed up, or not. I would have preferred to have been naked and wearing each other's sweat, wrapped in nothing more than sheets. The fundraiser didn't matter.

Right now, Sammy was the only thing that mattered.

She turned her head to continue gazing out the window. I was an idiot. If she was all that mattered to me, then why had Mother's words cut so sharply tonight?

Because I was still married. If there was ever to be anything more between us —damn, it if I didn't want more. I wanted her. I wanted a family with her and Xander.

"I expected you to be out all night," Danna said when we opened the door.

Xander ran up and hugged Sammy. She looked better almost right away.

"I wasn't feeling too good, so Alex brought me home," Sammy said.

"Why don't you go change, I'll take care of everything out here," I said to Sammy. "Do you need help going up the stairs?"

"No, the woozy feeling is mostly gone. Dana, I'll be right back." Sammy slowly began walking up to her bedroom.

"Hey," I said to Dana, "We haven't had dinner yet. Have you and Xander eaten?"

"We had chicken nuggets," Xander told me. He was already in his jammies, and looked ready for movies before bed.

"That's great. I'm going to go pick up some soup for Sammy. Will you stay here with her until I get back?"

"Yeah, sure. I can do that," Dana said.

Fortunately, Sammy didn't live too far from some chain stores. I picked up soups and crusty bread from a popular place that presented itself like a bakery, but probably sold more salads than pastries. I grabbed some ginger ale, and mint candies from the drug store. It had been a long time since I had a sour stomach, but those were the things that made me feel better.

Sammy was on the couch, curled up with Xander when I returned.

"I got you some chicken noodle soup," I told her.

"Thank you, you didn't have to do that."

I knew I didn't have to, that wasn't the point. "I want to take care of you, Sammy. Do you think you're getting out of our date so easily because you don't feel well?"

"Alex," she sighed.

"I'll go home when you go to bed."

I made sure Dana was paid, including for all the hours she was promised that didn't happen because of our early return.

We sat on the couch and had our soup, and watched the same cartoons with sharks that we watched when Sammy and Xander stayed with me at the lake house. I couldn't keep my eyes from drifting back to Sammy, making sure she was all right. And I couldn't stop thinking about how soon I could have divorce papers drawn up.

In the past six years of my marriage, I had never once thought about getting a divorce. And now, it couldn't happen fast enough.

# 21

# SAMMY

"**D**o you know what's going on?"

I looked up as Vanessa came into my office and sat in the chair across from my desk. I was in the middle of composing an email, and returned my attention to the words, but she looked angry. One eyebrow was pulled down and the other arched up toward her hair line. Her glasses were slim cat-eye shaped, so the arch in her brows was emphasized. Her lips were pursed, but the tell that something was really bothering her was how her lipstick was faded on her lower lip.

"Give me half a second, because I need to focus," I said as I finished typing. The email wasn't overly important, but it needed to go out, and I didn't want to forget to send it.

If I stopped now to talk with Vanessa, that would be a very real possibility. My ability to focus had been relatively scattered lately. As the mother to a young child, I had become a pro at multitasking. It was a requirement if I wanted to get anything done. But over the past few weeks, my attention was easily distracted, and then I would completely forget what I had been doing.

I hit send with a satisfied sigh and turned to face Vanessa. "Okay, what's the problem?" I splayed my hands on my desk and gave her all of my attention.

"I know you've been seeing Alex Stone. What I don't know is if you're actually dating, but..." She paused dramatically. "I figure you are talking to him about the business arrangement more than just in meetings and back and forth in emails."

I tried not to flinch or give anything away by grinning like an idiot or something. I was seeing Alex, a lot more than our business deal warranted. And we spoke about the actual arrangements substantially less than we should have. Business lunches were lunch dates where we stared at each other like love struck kids instead of hashing out the exact terms of this deal. We still hadn't determined if Foundation Network Communications was going to pursue a full buyout, or if they were going to simply acquire us and allow us to continue to do our thing.

I know I was angling for the second. I wanted to take Eyes On Care as far as it could go. I could envision expanding into other regions and being involved in other markets, not just childcare.

"I saw him a little over a week ago. We went to a gala fundraiser. I'm sorry, but we didn't really discuss business. He was too busy explaining how the wine tasting worked when I got sick," I told her.

The general malaise that had started from a case of extreme hurt feelings after overhearing the cruel things his mother and uncle were saying about me turned into a real case of something. My symptoms had bounced between those of a cold to those of a light flu. I felt generally unwell through the weekend into the following week.

Alex had been over at my house on and off through that time, constantly checking on me. And making sure that Xander had too much junk food. But the gala had been the last time our conversation had even come close to business.

She scrunched her face up more. "Did he hint at anything that might suggest they were going to change their minds?"

"What? No, what's happened Vanessa?"

She had more hands-on contact with Foundation Network Communications. They swapped the account information and handled such things as our case studies. Alex and I tended to talk about big picture items and how we envisioned the companies working together, while Vanessa and her contact did the actual work, providing the necessary documentation between the two companies.

"I got a call from Harper that they've decided to bring in a third-party auditing accountant," she said. "She's requested access to all of our financial records, going all the way back to the beginning."

That didn't sound bad to me. It made sense for them to audit our accounts. They had to see that we were actually making money. I shook my head. I didn't understand the problem.

"We've already been through this. Their team already reviewed our records. It feels like they found a reason or changed their mind to not continue with this deal." Vanessa compulsively licked and bit at her lip.

If she noticed a pattern, then definitely there was something, even if it was minor. I tried to think. Had something happened? Had Alex decided that merging our businesses would be a bad idea if we were involved?

I had told him at the beginning, when he was the one so eager to pursue me, that I could keep business and pleasure separate. Had that somehow changed?

"Sammy, we don't have the first two years' worth of records. They don't exist."

"Probably not. Did I know I was building a company? No, I thought I was building a network of babysitter swaps. They have to know that's the case. We have solid records after that. Are those records really that big of a deal?" I asked.

They weren't buying us in the past, they were dealing with us now. We had current records. We paid our workers and filed our taxes.

Vanessa shook her head. "I don't know. I think there might be something else going on here. Are you sure you didn't overhear anything? Alex didn't let anything slip when his guard was down?"

I narrowed my eyes and looked at her from the corner of my eye. What was she implying?

She let out a sign and rolled her eyes before crossing her arms. "You and Alex, there is something going on there. I can't figure out if it's an actual thing, or if maybe you're stalling so that you can keep his attention a little longer. He is rather attractive."

"Stalling? If anything, I should be rushing this through. I'm not the cause of this problem. I don't know if we are the kind of acquaintances where I could call him up and ask directly, but I will if you think that will help."

I was totally in a position to call Alex and ask anything regarding this arrangement. But I wasn't comfortable with Vanessa knowing that. His people needed to figure out which strategy they wanted to take. We had gone to them in good faith and presented ourselves as a worthy buy-out or partnership. Any delay was firmly their doing.

Her brows went up as if she didn't believe me.

"I'll call him. I'll ply him with drinks and my feminine wiles and see if I can seduce some insider trading details out of him." I thought humor might defuse Vanessa's suspicions a bit.

It seemed to work. Her distrustful expression slid away, and she seemed to relax.

"I know this has been your baby from the beginning," I started. "I fully agree with you, working with Foundation Network Communications would be so beneficial to us. No matter what capacity it happens in, I'm all for making it happen. We could use the investment to really take Eyes On Care places, and frankly, if they decided to buy us out and pay us off, that wouldn't be a bad deal either. Let me call Alex and see if he knows anything."

She twitched her mouth to the side. Her skepticism in my abilities all over her expression. "How about I sit here, and you call him?"

I shrugged. "Fine."

I pressed the intercom for the receptionist. "Hey, can you call Alex Stone's office for me?"

"I'll buzz you back when it's gone through."

I didn't typically have the receptionist make calls for me, but we had done it enough for her to know the routine. She called Alex's office, and then his secretary would either put us through, or let him know that we called.

It was the kind of power move top executives did with each other. It's how Alex had called me before I agreed to go out with him and gave him my cell number. It was also a way to let Alex know not to let it slip that there was something between us when he answered the phone.

"The call is going through now."

"This is Alex. What has you calling this afternoon, Sammy?" He sounded perfectly professional. There wasn't a hint of amusement in his tone.

"Hello, Alex. Yes. I have Vanessa with me." —another hint to not get personal on this call— "She's run into a situation with Harper. I'm sure it's nothing, but I wanted to seek some clarification."

I did my best to show all concern in my voice, this was my concern, my worry. I didn't want Vanessa to think that I didn't trust her, or that

I was blaming her for anything. She was already treating me as if I was being suspicious.

"I'll try my best, but Harper is tasked with carrying out certain items to move this forward," he said.

"That seems to be just it. She's requested some documentation for a third-party auditor. That feels like a back step. Can we confirm that it's more like a cha-cha, you know one step back two steps forward, than an actual reversal of anything?" I nodded at Vanessa to confirm I was asking for the information she needed for reassurance.

"Let me put you on hold."

Vanessa and I stared at each other in silence while we waited for Alex to return to the line.

"Are you there? Thanks for waiting. I just got off the line with Harper. Apparently, this request specifically came from the board. I think we can safely call it a dance step. There are several members of the board who are trying to speed this process up," he explained.

"This isn't speeding anything up," Vanessa snapped.

"I agree, but I also didn't see it as slowing us down very much either."

"Thank you, Alex. I think you have eased our concerns. We'll be certain to get the necessary paperwork to Harper." I ended the call.

Vanessa stood and smoothed down her pencil straight skirt. "I still don't like it," she said as she left my office.

# 22

## ALEX

I spent the weekend sorting through my personal files. When Red left my employment, he left everything neatly organized but it still didn't mean I would be able to locate anything that easily. His filing system wasn't a simple alphabetical A before B system.

Information was organized by themes. The vintage Shelby Mustang GT 350 was filed under C for car, not under Ford and not under Mustang. Even understanding the system, he had preferred, I still couldn't find any information for Abigail Sam.

I expected there to be some record of my marriage certificate. There had to be some kind of documentation. I found nothing. Not even anything under W for wife.

It was past time for me to file for a divorce. I would send flowers and a thank you card along with the papers. Abigail Sam had been a very useful wife, but now it was time for me to move on with my life. I couldn't do that while I still had a legal commitment with her. Wherever she may have ended up.

First thing Monday morning, Vanessa headed straight to Harper's office.

"Good morning, nice to see you," I said as I extended my hand to Vanessa.

I had been spending most of my time with Sammy when it came to discussing anything related to Eyes On Care.

"What brings you into our office this morning?"

She pressed the bright red frames of her glasses back up her nose. Her choice of eyewear was almost startling in its extremity. Every time I saw her, she wore a different pair.

Vanessa let out a delicate huff of aggravation through her nose. "Harper and I thought it would facilitate the transfer of certain documents if I were on site."

"As you know, the board has stepped in and expressed an interest in the acquisition process," Harper said.

I nodded. I had fought with Roy and my mother over the board's overreach. But they had convinced everyone that with a takeover this important they shouldn't be sitting back and waiting for me to deliver reports on a monthly basis.

They wanted an active role. Unfortunately, that meant they were making more work for everyone involved. Harper was doing a masterful job at keeping Eyes On Care as happy as she could. I might be surprised, but I wouldn't blame them if they soured on the whole idea and changed their mind.

If that happened, both companies would lose hundreds of manhours' worth of work. Foundation Network Communications would come away looking like we couldn't close a deal. Not a reputation I wanted to see us develop. And Eyes On Care would suddenly have the tech world's eyes on them.

If the board screwed this deal for us, they could be very well setting Eyes On Care up for a better arrangement. I wanted Sammy to succeed, but I wanted to be part of that success and not the chump who screwed it up.

"We appreciate you being willing to come in and humor the board of directors," I told Vanessa. "Harper will do her best to make everything run as smoothly as possible. Won't you, Harper?"

"Of course, as always. Now see, if I was your personal assistant and not here at corporate, I wouldn't be able to make sure that Vanessa doesn't get overly annoyed with us." Harper angled herself so that Vanessa couldn't see her face and gave me a manic wide-eyed grimace. Harper was equally annoyed by this interference.

I let out a heavy breath. "That's actually why I stopped by."

"Oh, don't mind me, I'll step out and grab some coffee. Want some?" Vanessa asked Harper.

Harper shook her head, and Vanessa left the office.

I stepped in close to Harper's desk and lowered my voice. "I need some help on a personal matter."

Harper let out an exasperated sigh and rolled her eyes. "How many times have I told you Alex, I'm not interested in being your personal keeper. Why haven't you hired someone?"

"Because I'm a grown up, and for the most part I can handle everything on my own. But Red had some valuable information, and I cannot for the life of me locate it in his records."

She shook her head. I understood the feeling. This should not have been this difficult.

"Why do you think I would know when Red had done with this information? Why don't you just call him or shoot him an email?" she asked.

"I tried. His email keeps sending back one of those out of the office replies, only for him it's out of civilization, we'll be back when we're back. I know, I shouldn't have let him leave without telling me exactly where everything was."

Harper let out a sharp laugh. "Alex, seriously? We are talking about Red. He totally told you where everything was. You were probably too busy pouting that he was leaving to properly pay attention."

"I don't pout," I said.

"Okay, boss. If you say so." She looked so disappointed in me. I think it actually hurt more to let Harper down than it was to be a failure in my mother's eyes. Harper actually knew what I was capable of, my mom not so much.

"Can you dig around and find out which lawyer has the details on my marriage," I asked.

"Oh, the mysterious wife makes an appearance," Harper said.

"Fuck, I hope not. I've lost track of her, and I think it's time to end that little arrangement."

"So, what is it exactly that you want me to do?" she asked.

"Find her. Find out where my marriage certificate is, and get me a divorce lawyer," I said.

"Oh, wow. A divorce. I kind of always assumed you would remain married to this mystery woman forever. To be honest Alex, I half didn't even believe you were really married. I mean..." she shrugged and made a face.

I knew exactly what she wasn't saying. I had never let my marriage stop me from seeing other women. Being married had only stopped me from seeing anyone seriously. And now that I was with a woman I wanted, my marriage was only in my way.

"What's your wife's name again?" Harper asked.

"Sam. Abigail Sam."

"Abigail-Sam? That's—"

Vanessa seemed to get stuck mid-thought as I turned to look at her. She had paused in the door frame, coffee in hand. She stared at me as if she were a goldfish, eyes large and round, mouth opening and closing but not making any noise. Suddenly she shook her head and came back to herself.

"That's a name. Who is it?" she asked as she slid back into the chair in front of her laptop.

"That's my wife's name," I admitted. There was no reason to hide or deny it, after all it was a matter of public record.

"I didn't know you were married," Vanessa said.

I shrugged. "We're mostly estranged. I have taken up far too much of your time this morning. Harper, will this be something you can handle?"

She nodded. "Yeah, I should be able to find out who has the information you're looking for. And while I'm at it, I'm going to have HR start finding you a personal assistant."

"If you did that, then what excuse would I have to come down to your office and ask impossible favors from you?" I joked. She was probably right; I should have someone to handle my non-business related personal matters.

I left her office and headed up the elevator to mine. I was bothered that Vanessa was here. She was a valuable asset to Eyes On Care. Having her here made us look like we didn't have our house in order. The board would never see that.

"Call Sammy," I said out loud.

"Calling Sammy Cole," the computer voice responded.

"Good morning, Alex," Sammy's warm voice said over speaker phone.

"Give me a sec, you're on speaker." I fumbled with my jacket, until I had my phone in my hand. I switched the call off speaker mode. "Good morning, I wanted to officially apologize for the nonsense the board is doing right now. Vanessa did not look pleased to be here."

"You saw her this morning?" Sammy asked.

"Yeah, she is working directly with Harper. I needed to meet with Harper briefly. I had no idea it had gotten to this level. I'll give them a call in a bit. I wanted to extend from one CEO to another. I understand this is redundant work and interfering more than helping."

"How exactly do you plan on demonstrating to Eyes On Care that this is an isolated incident?"

"Well," I dropped my voice and began thinking of all the ways I could show Sammy that I regretted what was happening. "I guess we could start by dinner out, you could see if Dana is available."

She laughed. "I'm going to stop you right there, Alex. On a personal note, I appreciate where you're going. But more seriously, your board does need to be made aware this feels like an overreach. Beyond that, I'm not actually prepared for this conversation at the moment. I trust that you have thoughts on this matter considering you reached out to me this morning."

"I'll talk to them. Hopefully they will see this as we do. Can I get back to that personal note? I missed you over the weekend. Can I see you tonight?"

"I missed you too. I can't tonight. I've got dinner with a friend I haven't seen in forever. She's in town and this was the only time she could get away."

"I understand," I said. I wasn't happy about it, but she was allowed to have friends. "Later in the week?"

"Let's see how I'm feeling. I've been so tired lately."

"Of course. Remember, I'm always good just to hang out and watch movies," I reminded her.

"I know you are. I really like that about you."

# 23

## SAMMY

Typically, when Vanessa came into my office for a chat, she would announce herself at the door, come in and sit down. It didn't matter what I was doing. She would wait, or chat and eventually work her way around to what she needed to tell me.

We had a very relaxed and familiar working relationship. So, when she didn't say a thing, and closed the door behind her and stood there scowling, I knew something was seriously wrong.

I still wasn't feeling perfectly well. I didn't have the energy to argue, or coddle, or make up excuses for whatever was bothering Vanessa.

"If the board at Foundation Network Communications has messed us up this badly, then I say we simply walk away from them," I said before she had a chance to say anything.

Maybe if she knew I was willing to walk before I allowed them to aggravate her further, she would not be so angry. And she was angry. Not annoyed but seething. I couldn't remember a time I had ever seen her like this.

"Abigail-Samantha, what the fuck do you think you're playing at?" She scolded me.

The tone, the clipped way she spoke my name brought back memories from my youth. Memories I thought were safely tucked away and forgotten. She sounded like my mother. My fight or flight nerves kicked in. Sweat formed on my upper lip and I shivered as all the small hair on my neck stuck out straight.

I shivered from the sudden panic, and as an involuntary reaction. My throat went dry as soon as I tried to swallow. I didn't know what I had done, just like when I had been a child. I didn't know what I had done then either. Only when I was a kid, I didn't understand that I didn't need to have done anything for my mother to turn on me.

Now, I was fully aware that I must have done something for someone to come at me with their aggression. Now, I was in a position to advocate for myself, and not sit there and be a victim.

I stood up. I was still shaking, but at least I knew I wasn't facing down my mother, only the shadow of a memory that Vanessa had triggered.

"Before you continue to scold me like a naughty child, you need to take a moment or ten," I said with a stern voice.

"The fuck I will. You're married to him. What the hell?"

I fell back into my chair with a thud. I blinked up at her. How had she found out? Alex didn't even realize who I was.

"I was in Harper's office, and they started talking about Abigail-Sam. Alex didn't even hesitate to say you were his wife. And don't try to deny it. How many Abigail-Sam's do you think are out there?"

I was stymied. I didn't know where to turn, or what to say. The panic Vanessa had triggered welled up inside of me. My stomach roiled. I tried to slowly breathe through my mouth. This entire situation was making me sick.

"Have you been sleeping with him?"

I held up my hand. "Let me explain."

"No, Sammy. You can't make up excuses to get out of this. Why didn't you tell me you were married to him when we started this whole thing? No wonder the board is requesting extra audits. What are the implications of merging the two companies when they are owned by the same couple?"

"It's not like that," I managed to say.

"Really? Then what is it? You're married to Alex Stone, why are we pretending that he knows nothing about this business? Did he help you before—" She pursed her lips together and glared at me. "You've been lying to us all. To everyone. You aren't some poor single mother who started this out of desperation. What a fucking lie. There goes any credibility we had!"

She spun and reached for the door. "I need to tell Cindy and Brad. They are going to be so pissed about this. Are we even going to get a payout when your little project gets absorbed back into the main business?"

"Stop!" I managed to cry out. Tears streamed down my cheeks. I was angry, humiliated, and hurt. How could Vanessa really think such things of me?

"It's not like that. He doesn't know it's me. We've been separated pretty much since the day after we got married." My mind was racing through what I could and couldn't tell Vanessa. I needed her to believe me, to trust me.

She barked out a sharp, disdainful laugh. "You're telling me your own husband doesn't know you are his wife?"

"I looked a lot different back then. I was a blonde, and I had short hair. I wore contacts. I've been waiting for him to figure out who I am, and he hasn't. Come on Vanessa, do you really think I'd live in a two-bedroom condo if Alex Stone was actively my husband?"

She didn't look like she believed me. She stood there with her arms folded, shaking her head.

"I don't get it. If you haven't seen him since you got married, why still be married? Why not get the marriage annulled or get a divorce? Sammy, make me understand what is going on here. Give me a reason to believe anything you tell me right now."

I let out a long slow breath. I didn't know how to explain this in a way that would make any sense.

"I don't know why you think you can't trust me. I have never lied. I am a single mother who started this business from a need. My husband has never been in the picture. We are married legally and that's it. And as far as I understand, there's some legal reason why we have to stay married. Before any of this happened, the last time I saw Alex Stone in person had been in a Las Vegas hotel room. I thought for certain he would recognize me the second we walked into his office."

Vanessa stood there staring at me. I couldn't tell if she believed anything I said or not. I wasn't lying, never had. My marriage status had never once been a topic of discussion. Married or not, my husband wasn't in the picture, leaving me a single mother.

"Are you stalling this? Is this some kind of personal vendetta against him then?"

Vanessa's question made no sense. Vendetta?

"Why would I have a vendetta against Alex or his company?"

She shrugged. "I don't know, you tell me."

I couldn't think of any reason. As it was, I could barely wrap my head around her anger. All I could do was stare at her in disbelief.

"That's it. I'm talking to Cindy and Brad. I want to see what they think of all of this."

As she turned toward my door again, I found a remnant of my personal fortitude. "Go ahead. It doesn't really matter what the three of you decide. This company is still mine. It's a sole proprietorship. You opted out of being in a partnership. At the end of the day, you are still just an employee. So are Brad and Cindy."

She spun on me viper fast. "Is that it? You're trying to sour this deal, so you won't have to pay out employee contribution percentages that you promised all of us?"

All of this time, I had thought Vanessa had been my friend. We had built this business together. I had wanted her to partner with me, but she hadn't wanted to. I had wanted to incorporate and divide the shares, but she had convinced me not to do that.

For the first time, I thought that maybe after all this time she had been right in making those decisions. My stomach lurched.

"Is that a threat against my employment?" she snapped at me.

"Take it for whatever you want. Just get out of my office."

She stormed out, taking years of partnership and friendship with her. When she left without dramatically quitting I had a glimmer of hope that she might come around. I sat and tried to focus and get my insides to settle down. My head was spinning, and my stomach complained in uncomfortable ways.

I closed my eyes and tried not to think. Holding still and focusing on my breathing didn't help. I reached for the trash can and retched. I rinsed my mouth with coffee before retching again.

I already wasn't feeling well. This was simply fantastic; I was so stressed that I was throwing up. I wasn't staying here any longer. I shut my computer down and grabbed my purse. I had to sit in my car until the nausea settled down and my head stopped spinning enough so that I felt safe enough to drive.

I gripped the steering wheel until my knuckles turned white. Mistakes had been made years ago. At the time I thought those actions were helping me, and now they were threatening my business, my friendships, everything.

If Vanessa reacted with such extreme vehemency because I was married to Alex, how the hell would Alex react when he found out who I really was to him.

I had to accept that I had been lying. I had lied to myself thinking I could do this, that I could be Sammy and leave Abigail-Sam and all of her memories and bad life choices behind. But I couldn't leave who I had been in the past, as much as I wanted to.

I needed to figure out what to tell Alex. This wasn't going to go well. My gut twisted at the thought. I had to pull over and throw up again.

# 24

# ALEX

"Hey boss," Harper's voice sounded through the phone speakers.

"Yes, Harper, what have you got for me?" I had waited an entire day for her to get back to me. This had better be the information I needed.

"I'm sending over the contact information for the legal team that has your prenup and marriage certificate. It took some doing, but I located them."

"What do you mean, located them? You make that sound like it was an ordeal. I guess Red didn't just use the legal team here?"

"He did not. It's an outside firm he had used before. If you think about it, it makes sense. In-house legal would know too much about your business. Anyway, Royce James is expecting your call. I was pretty much only able to confirm you did have business with them, but not what. And since I'm not you or Red, they were willing to give me their contact information and that was it."

I groaned.

"Sorry, it means you have to take the lead on this one. But the good news is, once filed, and the papers are signed, you should be a free man in two months."

"Two months? That's not too bad. How do you know it's only two months?"

"I looked it up," she confessed. "I know in some states there is no such thing as a quick divorce. And in some places the more you can pay the faster the divorce can be pushed through. I figured you would want to know how much extra this was going to cost you. Like I said the lawyer wouldn't actually talk to me, so I checked online. You'll probably want to confirm that with him. But from what I could find out, once the papers are signed it's sixty days."

Two months from signed papers. I was ready to sign the papers now, and they hadn't even been drawn up. Two months from locating my wife and getting her to sign and return the papers. It wasn't a particularly long time, but from where I was today, a married man, compared with where I wanted to be, not married and able to claim Sammy for my own, sixty days seemed like a very long time.

"Thanks, I'll give him a call," I said. I didn't want to wait a second, I wanted this to be done.

"Hey, Alex?" Harper asked before I could end the call.

"Yeah?"

"Are you certain your wife isn't going to contest this? You know, counter sue for alimony, drag this out for money?"

I chuckled. "No, she won't. The prenup is as solid as it gets. She agreed to a set payment when this would happen."

"So, you knew you were going to get divorced at some point?" Harper only asked questions when the information was pertinent to her work. But these questions seemed nosey.

153

"Thank you for the information, Harper." I told the computer to end the call. I didn't answer her questions.

"Call Human resources," I commanded the system.

"Calling Human Resources," the computerized voice said.

"Mr. Stone, what can I help you with this afternoon?"

"I'm checking on the status of a request that was put in. I need a personal assistant," I said.

"Let me transfer you to Marty. She's the one handling that for you."

I was placed on hold until a woman, I assumed was Marty, answered.

"Hello, Mr. Stone?"

"Where are we in the process of hiring my personal assistant?" I asked.

"I just received that request yesterday, Mr. Stone. I've reached out to two agencies in town to help us locate suitable candidates. Is there anything I should let the agencies be aware of? Are you in need of someone immediately? I can arrange for a temp." She sounded overly nervous and concerned.

"No, no. I wanted to check. Keep me informed of any progress, and I want to interview your top three candidates."

"Yes, sir. I will do that."

The call ended. I didn't normally step into a task I handed off. But something about Harper's questions annoyed me. She was probably simply being curious. After all, even though it was known around the office that I was married, my little coup ousting Roy from the office was no secret. But my wife was.

For at least a year, rumors about who she really was scattered through the office gossip mill. Conspiracy theories moved in waves across cubicles and up through the ranks. Had I really gotten married? Was there a secret child out there? Speculation that I married anyone from the daughter of some rich Texas oil robber baron to a supermodel who couldn't reveal she was married for contractual obligations ping-ponged through the gossip.

I ignored them all. Eventually the gossip dried up and stopped. Being married had more or less been forced on me to get my due. It didn't bother me that people tried to figure out what had really happened. There were three people who knew me, Red, and Abigail, and none of us were talking about it.

But now it was time to end that farce. The reasons behind my choices were nobody's business but my own.

I called the lawyer Harper had tracked down. The receptionist gave me a bit of a run around when it came to letting me speak to Royce James directly until I told her exactly who I was and why I was calling. It seemed like suddenly I went from no one bothering with the fact that I was married, to everyone knowing I was and that I was seeking a divorce.

"I'll connect you directly," she finally said.

"Mr. Stone, I haven't had the pleasure of dealing with you before. We always worked through your associate."

We did the perfunctory chit-chat of how Red was no longer working for me, and I had lost track of some important information, specifically that they were the firm that handled my prenup and were holding the marriage records. Royce went on to explain that based on the information Harper was able to provide he went ahead and had my records pulled.

"Your prenuptial agreement is very precise regarding expectations, should either party file for divorce. Since you are proceeding after the deadline in the agreement, there really shouldn't be any problems."

"How fast can you have documents drafted?" I asked.

"Getting the papers drafted isn't the issue here. We have contact information for your wife, but if it is not up to date, serving the papers may be a separate issue."

"If you have Abigail's old contact information, I'm sure one of your investigators can locate her current whereabouts," I said.

"Of course, that shouldn't be an issue."

I gave him the green light to proceed with drafting up the divorce agreement, and to engage an investigator to track my wife down.

"One other thing, I would like the papers to be delivered with some flowers and a thank you card."

"I'm sure we can handle that," the lawyer said.

I gave him the details and told him to give me a call when they had located her and had a timetable for delivering everything. With that done, I really only had one more hurdle.

I had to tell Sammy.

I had to let her know that I was getting a divorce and that I wanted to be with her. Something in me told me to wait. She didn't need to know I was filing for divorce just yet. I could wait and tell her when it was all done.

I didn't want her to blame herself for my divorce. The marriage was inconsequential at this point in my life. But Sammy was not.

I picked up the phone and called her. I didn't want her on speaker, I didn't want the computer to auto dial for me. Not for Sammy, she was too important.

"Hey Alex," she said as soon as she picked up the phone. She sounded tired, like she was still not feeling well.

"Are you feeling alright? How did your dinner with your friend go?"

"It didn't happen. I'm sicker than I thought, and then shit happened at the office. So right now, I'm doing damage control, and avoiding everyone because I don't want them to catch whatever this is that I have," she said.

"I'll bring soup. How's Xander? He isn't sick, is he?"

"No," she chuckled lightly. "He's got an immune system of forged steel. Healthy as a horse. It seems to just be me. I'm hoping it's food poisoning and not some tummy bug." She sighed. "It's probably best if you don't come over."

"Are you trying to get rid of me?" I teased.

"Alex, no, I'm…" she paused.

"I'm teasing. You aren't feeling well, are you?"

"No."

I thought I heard her sniffle. Was she crying?

"I won't stay but I will bring over some soup after work. I don't want you to worry about cooking. Do you need me to pick up Xander?"

"Alex." She was taking her time between words. "You aren't on the approved pick-up list. I appreciate the offer, but the daycare won't let you pick him up. Dana is on the list; I'll call to see if she can bring him home. So, thank you for the idea."

"Look, it's late enough in the afternoon and you could take off early, beat the traffic to your home. Get Dana to pick up Xander. I'll be over later with some dinner. Soup for you, and chicken nuggets for the kid."

"Alex…"

"Don't argue with me, woman. You don't feel well. Pushing yourself will only keep you sick for longer," I told her.

157

"You're right."

"Of course, I am," I chuckled. "I'll see you later when I bring dinner over."

I didn't need to stay, though I wanted to. I just needed to see her again.

# 25

## SAMMY

The annoying sounds of talk radio woke me from my dreams. The dream had been nicer than my current reality and I didn't want to get up. I wanted to drift back to sleep and find out what happened to the kitten that had found its way into the office. But the voices were obnoxious, and I wanted them to shut up.

With a torrent of cuss words, I rolled out of bed and crossed to where I kept my alarm. For years I had tried keeping my alarm next to my bed, but I had the bad habit of hitting snooze. I had been late for work far too often when someone suggested I move my alarm clock across the room.

I had been living with David at the time, and I didn't want to disturb him. So, I didn't move my alarm clock. I figured it wouldn't be worth the arguments at home. At least not until my job at the time was suddenly at risk. My boss at the time had told me that if I was late anymore, I'd be looking for a job.

So, I moved the alarm clock. Between not wanting to upset David and needing to turn the noise off for my own sanity, the alarm got me out of bed the first time I placed it across the room. I had been doing it that way ever since. It was a habit that wasn't hard to form, and now my alarm was always out of my reach, so I had to get out of bed to turn it off. I slapped at the button to make it stop. Immediately my stomach lurched.

I scurried for the bathroom. Other than the need to throw up, I felt fine. During the past few days, I had taken my temperature and I didn't have any fever. It didn't seem to matter what I ate; I'd be sick later. If this had started at the same time as Vanessa's melt down, I would have said extreme stress.

But the vomiting had been going on for over a week. I rinsed my mouth, washed my face and then decided I could risk brushing my teeth. There were some mornings when the thought of putting a toothbrush into my mouth made me sick.

I opened Xander's door and turned on the light. He would start to wake up with the light. After I got breakfast started, I'd come back up and get him out of bed. But for now, I just leaned against his door jamb and stared at him. He was a sleeping angel. My little guy.

Vanessa knew about me and Alex. I had no way of knowing if she would go and tell Alex. She hadn't come into work yesterday, and when I had asked what her plans were, she said she was thinking.

I didn't know if that meant she was thinking about continuing her employment with me, or if she was going to tell my secrets. If she had figured out that I was Alex's estranged wife, had she figured out that Xander was his son? It seemed obvious to me, after all, I named him Xander after his father, Alexander.

No, I needed to tell Alex. And I should probably get it over with and tell him today. I went downstairs and started the coffee. I popped bread into the toaster. The smell had my stomach lurching again.

This constant nausea was going to make me nuts. I pushed around on my stomach to see if anything was tender. I always thought gall-bladder and appendix hurt when they went bad. It was the only reason I could think of for the constant puking. That or I was pregnant.

Oh, shit. I hadn't thought about that. Alex and I had been responsible, then again, that hadn't stopped me from getting pregnant the first time. Contraception failed all the time.

I ran back upstairs to my room and picked up my phone. I scrolled through my calendar and looked at my period tracker app. I hadn't noted anything for far too long. Seven weeks to be precise. I sank onto my bed and covered my mouth.

I didn't have any pregnancy tests laying around. Xander wasn't quite awake. I wasn't going to be able to think straight until I found out. I slipped into a pair of sweats and went to wake Xander up.

"Hey baby, let's get dressed and go out for breakfast, okay?" I could get him to daycare early, stop at a drugstore, and come home to take the test. I wasn't about to risk doing something like that at the office.

I would just have to be late today, if I bothered to go in.

Time moved glacially slow. All I could focus on was getting to a store and getting a test. But I had this child I needed to manage and get to daycare.

I stopped and stared at Xander and then down at my belly. It didn't look any different. Was there another baby in there? I was terrified, and excited. I hadn't even managed to tell Alex yet about his son, and I was certain that I was going to need to tell him about a second child too.

Xander thought this morning was great.

"I love biscuit sandwiches, Mama." He told me over and over again. I had to promise to try to learn how to make them before he would cooperate and go into his daycare.

As soon as he was safe, it felt like time hit fast forward speed. I didn't have any time before work. I purchased a pregnancy test and a chocolate bar and headed home.

Once I took the test, I couldn't focus enough to even change clothes, or call into work. I really should call in and let them know I was taking the morning off. Maybe I should just give up and work from home for the day. I was the boss, there was no reason why I couldn't just take the day off.

I looked at the timer on my phone. The test results were not ready to read yet. I ate the candy as slowly as I was capable of.

My phone rang. I jumped and squeaked as it startled me. I answered without looking at the caller ID.

"This is Sammy," I said as I answered.

"Is this Abigail- Samantha Cole?"

"It is. Who is this?" I asked.

"We have a delivery for you and wanted to know when it would be a good time."

"Can't you just leave it by my door?"

"No ma'am. We need a signature. Besides, it shouldn't be left out," they said.

"I'm home now, how long before you think you'd be delivering this? I can't wait around for a delivery window between noon and four kinds of nonsense."

"No ma'am, we could be there in twenty minutes depending on traffic."

"Fine, I can do that. I'll stay around," I told them.

"Thank you, ma'am." The call ended.

That was it, I was going to call in. Between the stress of waiting for the pregnancy test, the stress of wondering what Vanessa was planning, and now having to wait for a delivery, I was overwhelmed. Work was not going to happen.

I opened an email on my phone and sent out a quick note to everyone. I was taking the morning off. If I wasn't in the office by one, I wasn't coming in for the rest of the day. Everyone knew I hadn't been feeling my best lately, so this shouldn't have been a surprise to anyone.

I checked on the pregnancy test timer. I had one minute left before it buzzed. I stared at my phone and watched the count down. When it sounded, I turned the notification off, and did my best not to run into my bathroom.

There it was; the white and purple plastic pen looking test. I stepped up to it. My breath stopped as I held it in with all the strength I had. This was going to tell me my future with more accuracy than a psychic with a crystal ball.

I saw the lines. Two of them. I let out the breath, a sob followed.

Numbly I walked back to my bed and sat down. Not that I knew, I didn't feel relieved. There was no excitement, no remorse. I had to have been in shock. I was pregnant by Alex Stone, again.

I don't know how long I sat there staring at the test result before the doorbell rang. It rang a second time before I managed to stand up and start walking.

When they rang a third time I yelled. "Give me a minute to get down the stairs, will you?"

It wasn't as if I was waiting on the opposite side of the door for them to arrive. I yanked the door open. "I'm moving slow, geez," I complained.

I glowered at a bouquet of purple lilies and other flowers. "Oh, right delivery."

"You Abigail Samantha Cole?"

"That's me. Who are these from?" I reached out and took the flowers.

"There's a card. But there's also this." They handed me an envelope. "You've been served."

"What? Oh, the delivery, right. Hold on a sec." I turned to find my purse to tip them, but they were already leaving.

I carried the flowers in and put them on the dining table. They were very pretty and smelled amazing. There were two cards. One on a stand in the middle of the bouquet, and another in my hands. I opened the large one I held.

"Oh shit." I scanned over the documents. Dropping them on the table, I plucked the card from the flowers. It was a standard gift card with the word 'thanks' across the front in an illustrated script style. The note on the inside was a slip of paper cut from a printout. 'Thank you, it's time for us to move on. Have a good life. Signed Alex.'

I knew what I had to do. I picked up my phone.

"Are you busy? We need to talk. Can you come over? Sure, after work is fine, but now would be better. I'm at home."

# 26

## ALEX

I dropped everything and drove straight to Sammy's house. She didn't sound good over the phone. My heart pounded in my chest. I couldn't get to her fast enough.

She had been ill, and she wasn't at work. My mind raced through every scenario, what was it she needed to see me about? Absolutely nothing I could think of was good. My worries had me thinking about every possible bad thing that it could be, from Sammy wanting to end things between us, to Sammy being gravely ill.

A weight settled in my chest as I navigated my car through traffic. I tried not to think about something being seriously wrong with Sammy. Had her constant low-grade illness over the past few weeks been indicative of something more serious?

What if it wasn't her, what if something was wrong with Xander? That kid had wormed his way inside my emotions. I would be crushed. But Sammy would be destroyed.

My tires squealed as I slammed on the brakes as soon as I pulled into her driveway. I was out of the car and pounding my fist against the door before the engine had fully stopped.

She wasn't opening the door. "Sammy! Sammy!" I continued to pound. If I had to break the door down I would.

She yanked it open. "Geez, give me a second to walk across the room. What is it with people and my door this morning?" She looked up at me, exasperated.

I stepped in and reached out to pull her into my embrace.

She stopped me with a hand on the center of my chest. She pushed and stepped away from me. "Come in. Sit."

There were purple flowers in the center of her table. They looked expensive. My gut clenched, was there another man? Is that what this was about?

"Who sent you flowers?" My voice came out more like a growl than a simple question.

She turned and looked at me, her expression was blank. There was no emotion there.

"You did, or did you forget?"

My brow furrowed. What? I hadn't sent her flowers. I should have. "That wasn't me. Looks like you got someone else's flowers. They got the color right."

I sat. Relief over the flowers felt like a cool wash over my body. I was still on my nerve's edge waiting to hear what she needed to talk about.

She handed me a card. I opened it. My gut sank as I read the words.

"That lawyer fucked up." I crushed the card in my hands. "I don't know how he got your address mixed up with my wife's. This isn't how I meant to tell you. Look, Sammy. I figured you already knew I was married. Neither of us ever talked about it. But when you walked into my office to present a potential partnership, I figured you had researched the hell out of me and the company."

She turned and walked away from me.

"I should have made sure you knew. I've been estranged from my wife for years." I held up the crumpled card. "I never filed for divorce because I needed to hold onto a stupid position against the board. Well, my mother and Roy specifically."

I crossed the room and stood behind her. I wanted to put my hands on her hips and turn her until her breasts pressed against my chest. And then I could kiss her, and I could show her what I was feeling. She was more important to me than some power struggle within the ranks of my family and by extension the business.

"I want to be with you," I crooned. "I'm divorcing her so I can get my life back."

She turned, and we were close. Half an inch and our bodies would touch. I closed the space. She was warm and trembling. My arm slid around the small of her back, holding her to me.

She slapped a manilla envelope against my chest. "I thought you were smarter than this Alex."

With a twist she was out of my grasp and walking away. She sat in a chair, leaving no room for me next to her. She let out a derisive laugh.

"I thought you had to be playing me. That you maybe didn't care. I've been terrified this entire time, but—" she clenched her fist to her chest and blinked hard, looking up at the ceiling "— I have to realize you have been completely clueless as to who I really am."

I didn't understand what she was saying.

"You never could get my name right."

"Sammy?"

"Open it already. Read it."

I pulled out the papers and scanned over them. They were the divorce papers. "That idiot. Why the hell did he send all of this to you?"

She sighed deeply with disappointment at me.

"What's your wife's name, Alex?"

"Abigail Sam, why?"

She tilted her head to the side. "Read the document."

My eyes scanned over the papers again. I froze. What the fuck? No, her last name had been Sam not Cole. Not Abigail-Samantha... I lifted my eyes to Sammy.

Her stare was hard and unforgiving. "I love you, despite the fact you don't seem to know I am your wife. I have been the entire time. And I don't want to divorce you even though you always thought my first name was Abigail, and last name Sam."

I ran my hand over my face. "That's why you kept correcting me. All this time I thought you were just trying to remind me that you were not taking the name Stone. Fuck." I dropped onto the couch.

I stared at the papers in my hands, and then back up at Sammy. She was right, I didn't know who she was. If she hadn't bothered to remind me that we knew each other, what other secrets was she keeping from me.

"So, this is what you needed to talk to me about?" I held up the papers.

"Part of it." She continued to stare at me.

I felt her scrutiny and I didn't want it. She was just as culpable as I had been in all of this. More so. She had known she was my wife and she had misled me. She lured me in and played me.

I surged to my feet and stormed out of her condo.

"That's it? You're just going to walk away?" She called out after me.

I looked down at the crushed divorce papers in my hand. I turned and stomped back to where she stood. Tears glistened on her cheek. She wasn't going to manipulate me anymore.

I threw the wrinkled papers back at her. "Sign them. Sixty days and you can be free of me and my gullibility. Was this all you had been lying to me about? Or is there more?"

She shook her head, her eyes blazing with anger.

"I didn't lie to you, just like you didn't lie to me. Neither of us said anything so don't try to blame me for everything that happened. You're the one who pursued me."

I stepped in close and bit my teeth together. "I thought you would sell out cheaper if you thought I also wanted you as part of the bargain. Looks like I'm the one who got screwed."

I didn't stop the next time she called my name. I was done with Sammy, with Abigail-Samantha. What a stupid name. I slammed my car into reverse. As I was about to speed away, I pulled back into her driveway. And jumped out of the car.

She was still on her stoop, arms wrapped around herself as if she were the victim trying to comfort herself.

"And another thing," I snarled. "I don't want your company near mine. The deal is off. Figure out how to do it all on your own."

"I always have anyway!" She yelled at me as I left.

This time I didn't stop. I kept driving. I didn't know where I was going. I needed to get out of town, away. I wanted to put as much distance between me and that woman as I could.

"Call Harper," I said to the hands-free system in my car.

"Hey boss, what's up?"

"Situation changed regarding Eyes On Care. If Vanessa Marche is in the building, please have her escorted out."

"She's not here, but what the hell?" Harper asked.

"I don't I've more details at the moment, but I suspect we've been the target of a fraudulent scam. Some questionable practices coming out of Eyes On Care have come to my attention. Put all action on hold until we decide what the next steps are."

"Well, crap. I had been looking forward to working with them. Do you need me to set up a meeting with the team here?"

"No, I'm not in the office, and I don't have plans on coming back this afternoon. Put a freeze on everything. I'll be back when I can deal with it."

"Are you all right, Alex? You sound stressed."

"That's because I am fucking stressed. Do you think getting a divorce is easy? I did, but it's not, it's messy. And now I have to deal with a merger gone sour, and—" I pounded my frustration out against the steering wheel "— why does everything have to fall apart at once?"

A truck cut me off. I slammed on my brakes and hit the horn. "Learn to fucking drive! Asshole!"

"Alex, are you driving?" Harper asked.

"Yes. God dammit, doesn't anyone in Dallas know how to drive?"

"I should let you go—"

"Don't you dare end this call before I'm done talking to you," I snapped.

"Alex—"

"Don't," I barked. "Don't assume you know what is best for me right now."

Harper was silent.

"Well?" I yelled.

"I don't know what you want from me right now, Alex. I need for you to end this call and drive safe. I will go take care of the situation with

Eyes On Care. Should I reroute any calls from them to come to me, so that I can tell them we've had to put them on hold depending on some further investigation?"

"Do that. Yes." I ended the call. Once I got rid of the distraction of Harper telling me what to do, I downshifted. The car lowered as the speed increased. I swung around the truck and took the car up to one hundred in hopes I could outpace my problems.

# 27

## SAMMY

I watched in shock as Alex raced away from me. Well, that hadn't gone as I had planned. Some misguided glimmer of hope in my chest had hoped he would laugh it all off.

Surprise, I'm your wife. And then he would laugh at the insanity of it all. How he had secretly known who I was all this time, but he couldn't believe it. We should have been wrapped around each other crying happy tears with relief.

One strange and possibly stupid move six years ago had actually helped us to find our soul mates, and how fortuitous it all has been. What a crazy fluke that my business would find a home within the ranks of acquisitions his company was out there looking to make.

Fate was aligning us to be together. We were married, our businesses meshed well, and to top it all off with whipped cream and a cherry, we were like some kind of crazy sundae of destiny, and we were really well physically suited. Contraception had failed us not once, but twice.

Well, fate and destiny could screw itself. I was more alone now than I had been in the past six years since our wedding day. I had made a mistake that day. The mistake wasn't marrying a rich man for a financial payoff, it had been falling for him.

He had been, and he still was so handsome, and so charming. If I hadn't fallen for him the first time I met him, I would have fallen for him this time. I didn't know which was worse, to have been quietly miserable without him for years only to finally have him want me or have him never realize who I was.

It was all a fresh kind of hell. He was out there, and he hated me. It would crush Xander to never see Alex again. At least Xander had never known that Alex was his father. My son didn't have to lose his father a second time. This way he only lost the guy his mama had been dating.

I ran my hands over my middle. I had another baby that was going to need me to be both mother and father. I had really wanted a different outcome than the one I was faced with. This felt all too familiar. I had Alex for a moment before he saw me as nothing more than a mistake.

My stomach gurgled with hunger. I laughed. I would have expected it to grumble and have the need to throw up again, but no, I was hungry. After the morning I had, I really hadn't expected to have an appetite of any kind.

I made toast, and let my mind wander to stupid things like how bright the filaments on the toaster got, and wasn't energy cool? I buttered the toast and tried to find something else to keep my mind distracted. Not thinking about Alex was really hard.

I climbed the stairs to my room and curled up in the middle of my bed. I pulled the blankets around me and let go of everything I had been gripping tightly to hold my sanity in check. I sobbed as my heart finally dropped out of my chest and shattered into a million pieces around me. It was like so much broken glass, and I was in the middle of it all with bare feet. I couldn't move without getting cut. There was no safe way out of this misery.

I must have fallen asleep because the next thing I knew, my phone was ringing incessantly. I tried ignoring it, they could leave a message. But whoever it was, they just kept on calling and calling.

I tossed my covers aside and crawled out of bed. I sniffled and wiped my hand across my face. I was still damp with tears. I must have been crying in my sleep.

I found the phone and answered it. "This is Sammy." My voice sounded thick with all the crying.

"Hey girl, it's Cindy. We have a situation. You need to get down here."

"I'm not doing well, Cindy. Can this wait until tomorrow?"

"There might not be an Eyes On Care tomorrow if you don't get down here. Vanessa is stirring up some kind of revolt and spewing all kinds of conspiracy theories about how you never intended to go through with the deal with Foundation Network Communications."

I let out a sigh. "Fuck. Okay, I'll head in. But I'm not changing for this."

"I'll see you when you get here."

I ended the call. I washed my face and shoved my feet into some flip flops. I stopped at a drive-thru on my way in.

It was weird, as if the baby realized with all the sadness, I couldn't be sick too. Now I wanted to eat. I shouldn't have complained. It was good to not have to deal with morning sickness while I was suddenly thrust into a position of putting out business fires.

When I got to the office, it was exactly as Cindy had described it. Vanessa was rousting the troupe, convincing them that Eyes On Care had only days left to be in business.

She looked at me with wide eyes. Clearly, she hadn't expected me to show up.

"It's easy to convince people that I don't know what I'm doing when I'm not here, isn't it?" I said with more sharpness and authority than I felt.

"You've screwed the deal with Alex. We're never going to get a friendly buyout offer again," she snapped back at me.

I shrugged. "It would seem that something has soured Foundation Network Communications against us, but it has nothing to do with anything I've done." I spoke loudly enough that everyone who wanted to listen in could.

"There is no reason to assume that because this offer looks like it might not happen, that this company is in financial trouble. We were fiscally healthy before we approached them. That hasn't changed. Vanessa, you are telling lies that are intended to harm this company. I think you need to leave. And you need to keep your mouth shut or I will sue you for slander and defamation."

She pursed her perfectly red lips and glared at me. "You can't—"

I took a deep breath. I really hated that she felt this way. But I had no other choice. "I'm the sole owner of Eyes On Care. I can. You're fired, get out. Anyone who wants to follow her based on the stories she's been telling; I don't want you here. Go."

I saw a few people hesitate, and clearly change their minds and put their belongings back on their desks. She took a good portion of the marketing team with. That was going to hurt. But it was best they were gone and not here making trouble.

I waited until it looked like everyone who was going to leave left. "Okay. I don't know what she told you. But let me come clean on a few things. First of all, Eyes On Care is in a healthy financial position. We approached Foundation Network Communications because we saw them as a means to be able to fast track the growth opportunities we wanted to pursue. We can still expand into those dream markets; it will just take us a little longer on our own."

"She said you, um, you were having relations with Alex Stone and that's what all of this is about." I didn't see who spoke up, but it was good to get that out in the open.

"Alex Stone and I have a complicated history. We both agreed that whatever came between us personally was not going to impact the deal. I have upheld my end of that commitment. Now, apparently members of their board requested an additional audit at the same time, but completely unrelated to some unfortunate personal issues. If the deal between the two companies is called off, it's going to stem from either that audit, or Alex Stone's inability to keep business separate from his personal life. I know Vanessa thinks I threw a wrench into the works as some kind of personal attack on Alex, but that's definitely not what's going on here."

"If they called for an additional audit, what are they going to find?" someone else asked.

I shrugged. "You all know I started this out of desperation and not some sense of business acumen. I came at it from a tech perspective, not a business one. They will probably find that I was a bit crap at running a business for the first few years. But once I understood what I was doing, and was in a position to hire business managers, I did manage the stuff fairly well."

Whatever I said seemed to have everyone nodding and slowly returning to their cubicles. I thought we would be able to return to normal, or what normal would look like without Vanessa's brilliant mind for running this business. I was so angry at her, but I still missed her.

I was more sad than angry for a week. Because a week was all it took before I found out she had wormed her way into employment with Alex at Foundation Network Communications. Not only was she now working for him. She was feeding him information that positioned their company against Eyes On Care. She was manning the helm as they poised for a hostile takeover.

Ultimately the joke was on her. With all of the lies she spewed, someone took her seriously and called the tax board with information about us. Eyes On Care, and me personally, were now being investigated for tax fraud.

It wasn't true, none of it was. But now with the situation with Eyes On Care and the tax board, no one was getting bought out. Friendly or hostile. It wasn't happening.

# 28

## ALEX

I sat back in my chair. I couldn't help but be reminded of another time in this very conference room when Vanessa had been pitching to me. Only that time Sammy had been with her, and I had been distracted.

This time I wasn't distracted, I was angry. She knew the ins and outs of Eyes On Care. Harper had told me that we needed to bring her on board. I hadn't been convinced. I usually trusted Harper's judgement.

"As you can see, by leveraging your position in the market, you essentially force Eyes On Care to follow a specific path. They want to expand in two directions. It's a matter of determining which direction they are headed in first. Force her to take the path we want, and then simply undermine the market, and cut Sammy off and she'll get weakened."

"You mean Eyes On Care would weaken?" I growled. Sammy Cole may not have been my favorite person at the moment, but it didn't mean I wanted her destroyed. What I wanted was for her to sign the divorce papers and send them in.

Once she signed them, I would be free of her. One signature and two months is all it would take for me to feel like myself again. I let out an involuntary chuckle, and then covered it with a sudden coughing fit. Two weeks ago, and I was thinking about how in two months Sammy would be all mine, there would be nothing to keep us apart.

"What's to prevent them from simply taking another path in the same direction?" Harper asked.

She and Thomas were sitting on this one with me. As with the first pitch from Eyes On Care, I knew that my judgement was going to be distracted. Only this time I wouldn't be staring at Sammy's impressive bosom.

The more anyone spoke about that company, the more I wished I was staring at Sammy's magnificent breasts. She had been distractingly beautiful. Much like a poison dart frog. So much beauty, and yet so dangerous. I should have known better.

"What do you mean?" Vanessa asked.

I dropped my finger onto the middle of her presentation. "They expand in Houston, we somehow block it, they turn around and take this to Galveston."

"Eyes On Care is already in Houston and Galveston, they aren't in west Texas or anywhere outside the border." Vanessa sounded smug. Where they were wasn't the point.

"The point was, if they start focusing on taking this east, and we somehow block them from establishing a network in Jackson or New Orleans, what's to stop them from shrugging that off and heading north or west? Nothing." I let out a heavy breath.

Vanessa had the information, she really did. But she was thinking in such a narrow frame of reference. She was thinking in two dimensions, she needed to be thinking in four.

"I'm not fully convinced. Eyes On Care could very well just be the one that got away. Let's start reaching out and finding other options." I stood, physically announcing I was done with this meeting.

HR had an interview for me. I was still trying to find a personal assistant who I could trust to keep me more organized outside of work. I had other things to do other than contemplate what had driven Vanessa from being so enthusiastic about the company Sammy ran to trying to undermine everything it was trying to accomplish.

"I think he's just willing to let it go so he doesn't have to see Sammy. I don't blame him. I don't want to have anything to do with her either."

I overheard Vanessa say as I walked away. I stopped. Turning back toward the conference room, I contemplated saying something. But what the hell would I say? Vanessa was right, I didn't want to have anything to do with Sammy anymore.

If that was the case, then why was I thinking about her so much? Her beautiful face, and the way she moaned out my name when I made love to her haunted my dreams.

It would be best to just forget the recent past. Eyes On Care had potential but it hadn't worked out. Time to let it go and move on. Time for me to stop obsessing over what Sammy had been thinking. She had so many opportunities to tell me the truth, and she hadn't. Not once.

I headed back toward my office. A young woman sat across from my secretary's desk. I stopped in front of her. She looked too young to be able to handle too much. She was skinny and had big eyes. I couldn't help but think she looked like a fawn, with skinny legs and knobbly knees.

"I'm Alex Stone, are you my one o'clock?"

She jumped to her feet and cut her hand through the air like a karate jab as she stuck it out to me.

"Yes, sir, I'm Mandy Keyes. Nice to meet you." She bristled with enthusiasm.

I tilted my head. "Come on in."

I asked my questions and I assumed she answered them. I was distracted and had been that way for a while. I needed to get my head out of my ass and back in the game. And that meant that this wasn't working,

"I have to interrupt you there. I'm not sure this would be a good fit."

I immediately regretted my choice of words. Her eyes grew even wider, and tears welled along her lower lids.

Dammit. I handed her a tissue.

"Sorry," she sniffed. "It's been a bit of a trial getting a job, making it to an interview is even tougher. People take one look at me and make a bunch of assumptions and the next thing I'm doing is apologizing for wasting their time, when they didn't spend hours researching me the way I did them. You know nothing about me, you haven't heard a thing I've said but you've already made up your mind. I'm sorry for wasting my time."

She stood and with a nod walked out of my office. As she was leaving, Harper brushed past her.

"I guess I'm not interrupting," Harper said. "Look, you were pretty rude to Vanessa earlier. I figure you're not happy about something, the divorce got you down?"

I shook my head. "Why is Vanessa here? I get that she had a falling out with Sammy, but why is she so focused on us acquiring Eyes On Care. It doesn't make sense."

Harper sat in one of the chairs in the conversation cluster. "Do you want my real opinion?"

"Why else would I be asking for it?"

Harper signed. "Right now, Vanessa is here as a part time consultant. She is helping us to locate other companies we can partner with. She is great at creative thinking. When I suggested she join us in some more formal capacity, she declined."

"So? Maybe she feels guilty about switching teams."

Harper shook her head. "Look, I liked Vanessa as a person…"

My brows shot up; I noticed Harper used the past tense.

"Right now, she seems like she is out to stick it to Sammy more than anything else. I'm sorry for what happened between you and Sammy. I know it's not my place to really bring it up, but Vanessa is almost taking that personally."

"Were she and Sammy close?" I was hurt by Sammy's act of hiding information from me, but I didn't want her destroyed. I was angry, but I didn't have the need to seek revenge.

"They were best friends from what I gathered. Vanessa helped to make Eyes On Care what it is. It's just weird to watch her. She gets all glassy eyed and manic when she talks about taking them down."

"How long of a contract do we have with her?"

"There you are!" Vanessa said as she barged into my office.

"Vanessa."

Harper was suddenly on her feet. "What are you doing here?"

Vanessa had a crazed smile on her face. "Eyes On Care and Sammy are under investigation for tax fraud." She started laughing.

That made no sense. My team had been over her numbers. They would have caught any indication that their books weren't authentic. Hell, even the annoying auditor that Roy had insisted on hadn't found anything that would indicate partnering would be a bad idea.

"So, what does that mean for us?" I asked. My chest tightened. Sammy would be stressed out. I wanted to reach out to her, but what would I say? *'I'm still pissed at you, but you don't deserve this.'*

"For one thing—" Harper crossed her arms "— it means we can't do anything about Eyes On Care while they are being investigated. We might as well turn our focus elsewhere. Vanessa, why don't you start looking into other small, specialized networking platforms. I'm sure by the end of the week we can come up with a list. I'll let Thomas know. Maybe he can remember some of the contacts from last year's MTC Expo."

"Isn't he headed out to that conference in Austin at the end of the month?" I asked.

"I think he is," Harper said.

"What, you're just going to drop Eyes On Care like it never existed? You should be building a strategy to strike once the investigation is over and Sammy is fined or made to step down for fraud."

"No, Vanessa," I started. "Eyes On Care has their own shit to deal with right now, and if they are under investigation, then we don't want that kind of bad press to rub off on us."

"Alex, you're missing a prime chance to be able to go in and buy Sammy out for pennies on the dollar. This will destroy their value; you can snap them up for nothing. I can't believe you don't see this as something to be preparing for."

"And if Sammy isn't found guilty of anything" —which is what I believed— "then we would've wasted a lot of time. No, I think it's time to let go of Eyes On Care, and to leave Sammy alone."

Harper said something and the two of them left. Vanessa's reaction concerned me. I wasn't gleeful that Sammy was in trouble. From a business perspective, I should have been positioning us to step in, but I couldn't. I just couldn't hurt Sammy like that.

# 29

## SAMMY

I sat in the conference room at work. Archie Smith, my lawyer, sat next to me. I had used his services only a few times since the business took off. But it was nice to consider that I had him to call on.

We were waiting for the auditors from the state to come back from lunch. They had spent the morning looking through boxes and boxes worth of filing. Those boxes now lined the back wall of the room.

But not everything was in those boxes. I knew it, the auditors knew it.

"You don't have to be nervous," Archie said as I fidgeted.

"What if it's bad? They aren't going to drag me in front of a grand jury or something, are they?"

"Sammy, it's not going to be that bad."

Archie reached over and squeezed my arm. He knew exactly what I was thinking. When I was informed of this investigation, he was the first person I called. And the second thing I asked him about was suing Vanessa. If she thought she could spread lies about me and I wouldn't react, she was very wrong. I still didn't understand why she was taking everything so personally. It wasn't her private life that was being destroyed, flipped on its back and left like a tortoise in the desert.

"I have years' worth of records missing." I bit my lip nervously.

"That's hardly anything. These folks are used to going after companies with years and years of missing files. You have two years tops worth of missing information. To be honest I'm surprised they are even bothering to investigate you."

I shrugged. "I think it's someone trying to stick it to me. I told you how Vanessa sort of rallied the troops against me? This is related, I'm certain of it. Can I sue her for defamation of character?"

"Do you have witnesses? Can you prove she did it out of malice and an attempt to destroy your business?"

Archie had kindly suggested we get through the investigation and audit before considering pursuit of action against Vanessa. He was right, I didn't want to be spread too thin. I still had a little boy at home who needed me.

"Maybe. There were definitely witnesses."

The main auditor, a woman, tall with a formidable presence walked back into the conference room followed by her two assistants. They moved around her like minions.

Archie leaned in close. "Let's talk about Vanessa later."

I nodded in agreement.

"Ms. Cole, we thought you should be aware these proceedings are a direct result of what was considered a viable report of insider trading and tax fraud."

I nodded. "Vanessa," I hissed under my breath.

"We are missing quite a bit of your records. Our notes indicate you filed 'Doing Business As' statements three separate times. But you only have records for the entity Eyes On Care."

"Yeah, I had a hard time deciding what to call the company."

"So that gives us an official date, as it were, that we need to have records from, and you don't have that."

I shook my head. I knew I didn't have records. But I also hadn't had much in the way of income back then. I spent more than I made.

"Bank statements?" she asked.

"I remember taking notes during a webinar that I needed a separate bank account, but I didn't open one until I had employees to pay."

"We will need your personal records, credit card statements, and loans from that time period. Anything where you can show us spending and income from your business."

I swallowed hard. I didn't keep papers at that point in my life. I didn't know that I needed to.

I was given six weeks to locate and turn over the requested records.

"Your credit card companies should have access to those records, same with the bank. You might have to pay a document fee. Keep those receipts. Is there a reason why your bookkeeping went from practically non-existent to saving everything?"

She gestured at all of the filing boxes.

"I got a business manager. Before that I was flying by the seat of my pants, taking classes, struggling to find childcare for my toddler." I pointed at the boxes and grimaced. "That's when Vanessa started working for me and we started to turn a profit."

I had to excuse myself when they began taking the boxes out of the office. They would conduct the bulk of the audit at their offices. The initial phase was what she had called the discovery process. If they 'discovered' it looked like important documents were missing, I would be contacted and given the opportunity to provide the missing information.

I locked myself in the last stall of the women's restroom and cried. Everything had been going so well. It felt like all those years of struggle were finally behind me. I had trustworthy friends. I had a successful business that was on the verge of being something truly amazing. I had Alex.

And in one broad sweep of epic bad timing and loss of trust, it was gone. Vanessa was no longer supporting the dream. The company was under scrutiny. And Alex wanted a divorce.

I indulged in some self-pity for about as long as I thought it would take the auditor's minions to carry my boxes out to their van. I washed my face and walked back to the conference room where she and Archie were waiting for me.

She reached out and shook my hand. "Thank you for cooperating as fully as you have. That's not always the case."

Archie and I followed her team out. I let out a big sigh that sounded like a suppressed sob.

"What a relief," Archie said.

"What do you mean?" I asked. It was horrible, they were taking away my records. I had to convince my employees that everything was all right while the tax people searched for evidence of fraud. It didn't look good.

"They only took the boxes. They didn't take any of the computers or issue any subpoena. I told you, you're a small case for them. I've seen cases where they show up with a warrant and walk out with every-thing, including everyone's personal phones."

I shivered. "That sounds horrible."

"That's the level they will go to if they really suspect serious fraud."

I rubbed my upper arms, and we headed back inside.

"Have you had a chance to go over that other issue?" I asked.

"I have. Who else have you talked about your condition?" he asked as he looked very specifically at my midsection.

I wasn't showing yet. I wasn't going to show for a while, and even after I started to have an obvious baby bump, most people would simply assume I was putting on even more weight.

"I haven't told anyone other than my doctor." I bit my lip. "I still haven't sent in the papers." I admitted.

After it felt like my world imploded around me, and I was able to crawl back onto my feet again, I had asked Archie to read over the divorce papers. I provided him with a copy of the prenup. I wanted to make sure everything was going to go smoothly. But mostly I wanted to make sure Alex didn't have a clause or a tricky word in there that would give him custody of any children.

Archie assured me that there was nothing in either document about offspring. "You need to send that in, Sammy. Holding onto it doesn't mean you can't be divorced. He'll be able to say he made a good effort to contact you, and that you were properly served. Your lack of action doesn't stop anything. It simply drags it out longer."

He was right. Holding onto the divorce papers wouldn't magically make Alex come back to me. And why would I want him? For all the same reasons I hadn't stopped thinking about him after the very first time I met. I had fallen in love with my husband.

I shouldn't harbor those feelings. He was certain to be out for my business. I could just imagine Vanessa rubbing her hands together and cackling as she led the charge right behind Alex to attack and take over my company like some charging invasion horde. I let out a soft laugh as I imagined Vanessa in her stylish business wear carrying a spear and shield like a Viking.

Archie was right. I needed to sign and send in the papers and get that part of my life behind me.

"So, I take it you don't plan on pursuing any form of child support from him? You know the courts could make sure he takes care of you very well. You have proof that you were married, and he abandoned you."

"We were estranged," I corrected.

"Not from what you mentioned. He decorated a room for Xander at his lake house. You may have been estranged, but his actions of the past few months sound very much like the two of you reconciled. Sammy, you're pregnant. On paper, that looks a lot like a reconciliation."

"It would be so hard on Xander. He's such a delicately nurtured child. To find out his father abandoned him would break his little heart."

"You don't have to tell him," Archie said.

"What should I tell him when they stick needles in him to take DNA for the paternity test?"

Archie chuckled. "That's not how that works. They use a long cotton swab and scrape the inside of his little cheek. It doesn't hurt."

"No, I don't want to go after Alex for child support. If I did, that would give him an opportunity to take my kids away, and I won't allow that. I've survived without any child support from him for the past five years, I can keep doing it."

"Two kids aren't cheap," Archie mentioned.

"Maybe not, but I'm the CEO and founder of an up-and-coming tech company. I can make my own money."

"I believe that you can, and that you will, Sammy." He patted me on the back. It felt as if he were humoring me more than believing in me.

## 30

---

# ALEX

One of the qualities of being a good leader is listening, actually listening to the people that have been trusted to do certain jobs. It's pointless to delegate if in the end the advice of others is ignored.

A good leader provides mentorship and advice. And surrounds themselves with smart, experienced individuals, and listens to the counsel of others.

I hired smart people and put them in strategic positions for a reason. I needed to be able to trust their judgement. And I needed to separate my feelings from what was good for my business.

I didn't like the idea of positioning Foundation Network Communications to swoop in like a vulture on Eyes On Care when their company was at its most vulnerable. I wanted Sammy out of my life and the best way I could figure out how to do that was to leave her, and her business alone.

My team felt otherwise. And with Eyes On Care's tax audit having put a hold on all activity outside of the standard day-to-day operations, my team had the time they needed to convince me that I was not thinking clearly.

Vanessa no longer had a connection inside the walls at Eyes On Care. We didn't have a reliable source for insider information, so we had to watch what was public record, and follow the actions of their business carefully.

Since Vanessa had spent years working closely with their CEO, she was the one to gather that information for her reports. Thomas tracked market value, and the financial position of the company. Harper filled in the gaps. As a team they were a finely honed instrument.

"I don't like how quickly this looks like it's happening," Thomas said.

Once everyone managed to get me back on board to follow through with a take-over, we began meeting every other week. The thought process had been that a weekly meeting would be overkill, especially since an audit like theirs could drag out for months. Meeting every other week would cover our asses in case the situation began to change rapidly.

"What do you mean?" Harper asked. She crossed my office and began poking at the spread of sandwiches and sides that had been ordered in for lunch.

The session was informal. We discussed strategies, and observations over lunch. It gave me a chance to sit back and observe from a more comfortable position. Also, the banter and conversation seemed to flow more organically when food was involved.

"I mean that it seems like the audit is either over or almost over. Following the trades and reports Eyes On Care is holding stable. Industry analyst reports show that confidence in the company is solid."

"Solid but weak," Vanessa said.

"No." Thomas leaned across the coffee table in the center of my office and showed a printout to her. "Not weak at all. We should have seen a second dip by now. There was an initial dip when the audit process began. Confidence in the company dropped. But they recovered."

"Isn't that expected? Initial drops occur when people are freaking out, but if nothing seems to happen those data points return to their initial positions," Harper said.

"Of course, as expected. But then with a drawn-out process such as this, people are going to start getting nervous. They want to know what's happening. With any kind of drawn-out investigation those numbers drop again with either a rapid recovery when positive outcomes are announced, or taking a hard hit with bad news," he continued to explain.

"Sounds like they're just in the middle of something drawn out. I wouldn't worry about it. They haven't taken that final hit yet."

Vanessa chuckled. "But they will, and that's when we strike."

"Do we have the offer ready to go?" I asked.

"We have several depending on what the results of the audit show. If it's so bad that Sammy has to sell in order to keep the company afloat, which is what I am counting on, we can come in with a super low offer," Vanessa said.

"If she has to step down, are you so certain she won't just fold the whole thing and shut it down?" Harper asked.

"She loves what she started. That company is as much her baby as Xander is. Maybe more so, she was able to spawn on her own without some one-night oopsie setting her up."

I shot Vanessa a glare, and then looked away before anyone noticed my reaction. Sammy wasn't my favorite person, but I still felt possessive when it came to people speaking unkindly about her. It was messed up, but I wanted to snap at Vanessa. How dare she impugn

Sammy or Xander? Xander had nothing to do with any of this. He was innocent, he shouldn't be included in any of the discussions about his mother's business. Not even as some adjacent throw away comments.

The growl I felt stayed in my throat. I would still protect that child from the world, even if his mother and I were not together.

"Oh, sandwiches. Is there enough for me?" My new personal assistant Mandy said as she walked into my office.

She had been right about a lot of things during our interview. I made assumptions, but I had listened. And when she left, she revealed a tidbit of information, that had I been in the right frame of mind at the time, I would have latched onto. As it was, it took me a few days to have my secretary call her back for another interview.

Mandy Keyes had done her homework. She knew more about me than my mother might have. We agreed to a trial period of ninety days before either of us decided this was or was not going to work out. So far in her first month of employment, she had proven to be just what I needed.

She filled a plate with food and sat next to me. She handed over a legal-size manila envelope.

"You've been waiting for this, I believe," she said.

I took the envelope and opened the flap. I glanced inside. My gut clenched when I realized what I was looking at. I set it aside and turned my focus back to the discussion at hand. Only that wasn't working for me.

"She'll probably be really grateful we show up with a cash offer," Thomas was saying.

At some point I lost track of the conversation. Fortunately, the purpose of this lunch meeting was solely focused on the acquisition of Eyes On Care, so I couldn't get too lost. I didn't have to ask who would be open to a cash offer, it was Sammy. It was always Sammy we were talking about. Every comment, every strategy was a character assassination against Sammy.

My eyes kept returning to the envelope. Mandy noticed and nodded in its direction; her eyebrows raised in curiosity. I shook my head in a silent comment. 'It's nothing, don't worry about it.'

To make it clear that the contents of the envelope meant nothing, I casually handed it back to Mandy. "Drop this on my desk."

"Your desk is literally eight feet behind you and I'm eating." She wasn't one to bandy about. I wasn't sure if that was an enduring trait or one that would piss me off in the future. I had two more months to make up my mind about hiring her full time.

I got up and dropped the envelope on my desk. I took the opportunity to stretch.

"She doesn't have any kind of records for the first two years of business, I can't see how they aren't going to let her get away with that."

I groaned. This meeting was following the same pattern the other ones had. Maybe lunch was too much, dragging the time out. Once we had discussed new information, and reviewed data points, the chatter all dwelled back to how bad Sammy was at business, how the only reason Eyes On Care got as far as it did was because of Vanessa, and she was with us now.

Sammy was eviscerated every time. My Sammy. That beautiful, charming, sweet woman was torn apart as if she weren't a real person but a commodity to be traded, and downgraded.

I glanced back at the envelope. She wasn't mine anymore. The papers in that envelope were the last nails in the coffin of our relationship. She finally signed the divorce papers.

"You know what? We're done. I'm done. You aren't saying anything new. Sammy Cole may be a lot of things, but she's never been the malicious businesswoman you are making her out to be."

"Are you second guessing this takeover, Alex?" Harper asked.

"Maybe I am. Or maybe I'm getting sick of hearing you talk about someone who only a few months ago we all treated like a friend."

"Someone who betrayed us," Vanessa said.

"Did she really? Because you worked for her, and now you're telling us strategies and plans that her company implemented. I'm not sure if she betrayed me, not really."

I turned back to my desk, grabbed the envelope with the divorce papers and stormed out. Just a few crushed pages in my hand, and my entire world had changed. I had thought it would be for the better, but all I wanted was to take these papers and shred them. I wanted to watch them burn. And I wanted to do that with my arms wrapped around Sammy's soft warm body.

A good leader listened to his advisors. He also admitted it when he fucked up.

# SAMMY

Another meeting, another conference room. This time I sat in the state tax office's conference room. The room itself wasn't very nice. There wasn't a glass wall like the one in my office. This felt more like a holding cell, only there were windows to the outside. The view was the back of another low concrete city government building.

Archie came with me because I was so nervous. I had managed to get the auditors all of the documents they wanted within three weeks, beating their deadline. I had to beg my credit card company for copies of my card statements for the first three years after I had started Eyes On Care.

After I turned the last bank statements over, I waited. The auditors didn't ask me for anything else and said they would contact me. And then they didn't call. I panicked. Why wasn't I hearing from them?

I didn't have information I could share with what staff I had left. And every week that number seemed to be smaller and smaller.

Archie sat next to me and occasionally would reach over and tap my shoulder. I couldn't decide if it was a condescending gesture or a legitimate attempt at calming my nerves. He was easily as old as I imagined my grandfather would have been, so maybe a little bit of both, calming the crazy lady.

The auditor and her minions sat across from us. She was less stern than I remembered. And her minions looked like they were bored. She slid a file folder of papers across the table toward me. "We are returning the documents you provided, this is an inventory."

I reached out and pulled the file folder toward me. I wasn't prepared to carry boxes back to the office. I had been mentally preparing to be arrested or something overly dramatic.

A single sheet of paper was slid toward me. "If you could sign indicating the paperwork has been returned," one of the minions said.

I glanced over at Archie. I was confused. He was grinning. I hoped that meant good news. I accepted a pen and scrawled my signature.

"Your record keeping for the initial years of your business is a mess," she said.

"I know," I confessed. "I didn't know what I was doing."

"Obviously." A snicker of suppressed laughter bounced between the auditors.

"That bad?" I asked. I knew the answer was yes.

"It is. We did find one small error that you repeated a few times."

I gulped. What was their definition of small? I grimaced. I was prepared for a fine. "What's the damage?"

"You underpaid the state one hundred thirty-five dollars and forty-three cents."

"What?" I asked.

She nodded at the file folder. On top was a statement, I read over it. I owed less than two hundred dollars. All that stress, all that uncertainty and it came down to my grocery budget.

I glanced at Archie. He smiled and nodded some more.

"I didn't bring my check book," I confessed.

"That's fine, you can pay the clerk on your way out. I think they take credit cards."

"What am I supposed to do with all of my boxes? I didn't realize I was going to have to move them all back."

"Don't worry about that," Archie started. "I'll have someone back at the office make arrangements for you."

"Thank you." I felt like I was floating through a dream as the meeting wrapped up, and Archie guided me through the building to the clerk's office. Everything felt surreal.

I wasn't going to be arrested, there was no reason to assume my company was going to fold. I had thought about it more than once. And I'm sure my employees had as well.

I lost two more of them last week. Maybe this would be seen as a sign, and we could start to turn everything around. We still had market share; we were still solid. But if another hit was coming, Eyes On Care wouldn't survive.

Maybe I should sell it. I could sell and move to Silicon Valley and the center of the tech world. I was smart enough that I could get picked up by a start-up, or brought into a more established company. Maybe I could go to work for one of the big boys and become an anonymous hive worker that no one would expect much more from me than my assigned tasks.

Some decisions needed to be made. And I was the one to make them. I think I would start by searching for a new COO and business manager. That should show everyone that Eyes On Care was down but not out.

I let out a big sigh. "What a relief." I gave Archie a weary smile. "Even though I ended up not being at any kind of fault here, can I still sue Vanessa for trauma?"

"Are you sure you want to do that? This was six weeks of relatively low stakes stress. Proving a slander case takes a lot of work. You need to have witnesses who are willing to come forward. You have to prove financially how her lies impacted you."

"I lost a lot of sleep and a lot of work hours digging up information for the auditors." I pointed out.

"Seems to me the state would have a better case against her than you would. That is if they even knew it was her who tipped them off. They had three people working on your case for six weeks. And, assuming they were on your case alone, that's—" he quickly calculated on his fingers "— three hundred sixty working, no, wait, seven twenty, seven hundred and twenty working hours. Even if the three of them worked on your case a third of the time that's still over two-hundred-man hours. Your case cost the state much more than they recovered with that measly one-thirty-five."

"And forty-five cents," I added. I let out a disappointed breath of air.

Archie was right, it probably wasn't worth my time going after Vanessa.

"Celebratory drink?" he asked.

"Definitely."

At the restaurant Archie drove to, he ordered a jack on the rocks, and sparkling lemonade for me. Of course, Archie had known. I told him when it came to reviewing my divorce documents. But it was pretty obvious by now that I was pregnant again. At only three months I was showing much more dramatically than I had anticipated.

We toasted and clinked glasses to our successful survival of the audit.

"Now how's your other situation?" he asked, nodding at my middle.

I bit my lip. "I sent in the papers." I admitted. "But I haven't heard anything. Shouldn't the other lawyer let me know they've been filed or something?"

"I'm not a divorce lawyer, but yes, you should have received some form of notification that the papers have been filed. I can have someone in the office check on that for you."

Archie had someone in the office who could check on, follow through, and investigate anything. He paid them more than enough to be able to do, or more likely willing to take care of all the little things that needed doing. I needed to get someone like that.

Especially now that I was expecting a second baby. Alex had a butler type assistant when I first met him. That man had taken care of some many little details. But that was his job, take care of the little things so the boss could do the boss things.

"How would I go about getting a personal assistant?" I blurted out. "I want to have 'someone at the office' who can do the things."

"What things?" Archie asked.

"Well, so far you've got someone who can follow up with some agency to see if my divorce has been filed. And you have someone who can arrange for my files to be picked out from the auditor's office and returned to mine. I want that. My business isn't going to fold any time soon. Maybe that's my cosmic hint to start acting like a CEO?"

Archie smiled, and then started to chuckle.

"Let me guess, you have someone at the office you can ask about that?" I chuckled.

"Exactly. Now that you know Eyes On Care is not in danger from some kind of tax chopping block, what are your plans?"

I shrugged. "I've got a lot of damage control to take care of. Employee confidence has been dangerously low. This outcome should turn that around. I'm still without a business manager and COO. I never realized how much Vanessa really did to help me until she was gone. I'll take this time to really analyze where we can streamline our workflows. Do I need to rehire everyone who left, or can we do something to refine the team?"

I sat back and sighed. "I need to do something to reward the people who stuck around. The ship didn't sink, but the rats certainly left as if it were."

Archie raised a bushy brow in my direction.

"Okay, maybe calling my ex-employee a rat isn't very generous of me. But they ran away and didn't stick it out. Feels very rat-like to me."

"I don't think preserving one's livelihood is rat-like behavior. I know it feels personal. The company is personal. I think maybe now would be the time to properly incorporate it. You'll be able to court more investors, and your personal income and assets will not be on the line."

I reflected for a moment about how different all of this would have been if Eyes On Care had been incorporated properly. As it was, everything financially had fallen on my shoulders. That financial burden was why Vanessa hadn't been interested in being a part owner.

I added it to my mental list. When I got back to the office, I was going to have to transfer all of these ideas onto paper.

# 32

## ALEX

I drove for hours. I didn't have a destination in mind, I just wanted to get away from everything that had gone wrong. And it felt like everything had gone wrong. Working with my team smacked too much of dealing with Roy and my mom. Go after the little guy, do it fast, make it hurt. That's not what I had wanted.

I had wanted to build trust, and a relationship, not only with Sammy, but her company. Vanessa made it feel like we had a vendetta to enact. Retribution. And it was wrong. All of it.

I drove until there were no buildings and the sun sank below the horizon. Headlights flared on, and I continued to drive in the dark. I drove fast. As if speed would provide me with the desired comfort from my pain and emotions.

At some point I pulled over into a truck stop and slept in my car. It always struck me as weird, this entirely different lifestyle. People drove to get from place to place. Truck drivers hauled goods and lived off the food that truck stops sold.

I always flew over it. Destination to destination. I didn't do this in between stuff. I didn't have the time for it. But it was a place to run to. Where did these people go when they needed an escape?

In the morning, I stumbled inside and got a coffee and a questionable burrito. As far as junk food went, it wasn't too bad. It reminded me of eating Taco Bell after a late night of drinking in my college days. I sat and stared out at the vast landscape of Texas. It looked as empty as I felt. Vast, barren, abandoned, and lonely.

A guy could get lost here and wander for years. Maybe that's what I needed to do, to get lost in the wild. I took a sip of the coffee and a bite of the burrito and realized I would not survive without civilization.

I glanced at the envelope on my passenger seat. I didn't need to get lost in a harsh environment to be alone. I had taken care of that. I started the engine and headed east, back toward home. I bypassed town and went to the lake.

When I opened the door and disarmed the alarm, I realized this may have been a mistake. Evidence of Sammy and Xander was everywhere.

I opened the fridge and grabbed a beer. There wasn't much else in there other than some condiments, and juice boxes. Grabbing a second beer, I then headed through the back doors, out to the back and to the dock. I sat, removed my shoes and socks and dropped my feet into the water.

The beauty of my surroundings was lost on me. I felt more at ease when surrounded by scrub brush or barely anything green, yet I had returned to the water for solace. I was a mess and had no idea what I wanted, or where I was going.

My phone vibrated and I picked it up. Another text from Mandy. She had been blowing my phone up ever since I walked out.

"I'm alive, leave me the fuck alone." I tapped out with my thumbs.

"Send beer, pizza." I sent another text and my address.

I looked over my shoulder. I kept expecting Xander to come running out with his crazy bright life vest on. Sammy had been too much, too paranoid. She didn't want him playing near the water without his vest on.

I guess I was going to have to put the swing set in the front yard. But nobody did that. "Fuck." I didn't need to do that. There was no need for a swing set, no kid. No family. They had been here enough to infuse this place with the ghosts of their laughter, their memories and joy filled the place. Even though their time here was brief, it had been our home.

This divorce felt real. I hadn't anticipated that. After all, nothing about this marriage had been real. I had a wife of convenience, on paper only. This divorce was nothing more than signatures on paper. So why did it leave me empty? My life with Sammy and Xander had been more real than any of it, and at the time I had been too stupid to realize they were my family. And those papers in that envelope brought it all crashing down.

I flipped through pictures on my phone. I still had them all. In my anger I couldn't stand to look at a reminder of Sammy, so I simply ignored her pictures. In moments of doubt, and confusion, I found myself looking at her again, and again.

I wanted to do little more than stare at how her cheeks curved and rounded when she smiled. What was wrong with me? I needed to delete these pictures.

My thumb scrolled right, yes, I needed to stop thinking about her. Get her out of my mind, off my phone. My thumb hovered over the trashcan icon. I couldn't. My fingers were paralyzed. Half an inch down was all that needed to happen to make that picture go away.

But I didn't want it to go. She was so beautiful, a smattering of freckles across a sunburned nose. Laughter in her eyes. The picture made me relive that moment. A moment where we were happy, all of us. Life had been good. I didn't want to lose that.

I swiped and a picture of me as a kid filled the screen. How the hell did that get there? I shouldn't have any pictures from my childhood on my phone. Had my mom sent it?

I sat up and stared at the image. It wasn't me; it was Xander.

"Holy Shit."

My phone buzzed and a dropdown notification covered the photo. My pizza was here.

"OMW" I texted. I pushed up to my feet, and crossed through the house until I opened the door.

The delivery guy brought in a stack of three pizzas. I pulled a twenty from my wallet and handed it over.

"Where's my beer?" I asked.

"I don't deliver beer, man. Just pizza." He took the tip money and headed out past another delivery driver.

"I got your beer," the second guy said.

"Bring it in," I told the second delivery kid. I handed him a twenty.

Mandy had done well, both items were delivered at almost the exact same time.

I put the beer in the fridge and checked out the pizza. There was a note across the top box. 'Didn't know what you wanted. Got a variety.'

Mandy was thinking ahead, including having the delivery write a note on the box.

I picked up a piece from the top box and took a bite. Hungrier than I realized, I grabbed another beer and leaned on the kitchen counter.

I sent the picture of Xander to my mother. "Look familiar?"

"Get me birth records for Xander Cole," I texted Mandy next.

"You mean Sammy Cole's kid?"

"Yes, I mean Sammy Cole's kid. He should be about five."

"Why?"

It was none of her business, why. "Just do it."

My phone rang. "Hello Mom," I said as I picked it up.

"Why are you sending me old pictures? Is there something I should remember about this one?" She had a lot of questions.

"That's me, right?" I asked. I needed to know I wasn't the only one suddenly seeing this. "But with lighter hair."

"Yes, that's you. Your hair didn't turn dark until you started school. You were even blonder when you were a tiny baby."

"Could it have been from Dad taking me to the zoo?" I asked.

"He did that kind of thing all the time, I suppose so," she said. "Why?"

"I found this, but the hair threw me off. I guess it's been a long time since I looked at old pictures," I said.

"You were such a cute little boy. You would make beautiful children. When are you and your mysterious wife going to give me grand-children?"

I ended the call. I didn't want that particular conversation. I didn't know how to tell her that my wife and I had already given her a grandchild, only I was too wrapped up in myself to have realized it. At least I was fairly certain we had.

Grabbing another slice of pizza, I went back to scrolling through photos. This time I focused on Xander. He looked too much like me for it to be a coincidence. I was a fucking idiot. His name was Xander. A derivative of Alexander. And somehow, I completely missed that. Stupid. Stupid. Stupid.

I was supposed to be smarter than this. I should have been smart enough to recognize Sammy with different hair, and glasses instead of contacts. But I hadn't. I had barely looked at her with a sober brain on the day we got married. She was attractive, she was my type, that's all that mattered at that point.

Why hadn't meeting her again tripped those alarms in my brain? Because I wasn't looking for my wife to show up in my conference room. I wasn't looking for my wife when I kissed her or seduced her. And I certainly wasn't expecting her child to be my son.

"I can't find much." Mandy texted. "But from her Facebook page it looks like his birthday is in January. I'll need more time to see what I can dig up in official records. It's harder with kids."

January. I counted back on my fingers. I knew our anniversary because I remembered the day I forced Roy to retire, and not for any other reason. Of course, I could confirm the date from the papers in that fucking envelop. But I didn't need to see Sammy's signature agreeing to end our marriage, and also to see that we were married in April.

"Fuck, I have a son."

# 33

## SAMMY

The doorbell rang, followed by a knock. I understood my place was small, but why didn't people understand that I didn't sit and hover by my front door just waiting to open it?

I grumbled, "Give me a minute" and started to work my way out of the comfort of the couch like some kind of beached seal trying to get off a rock at low tide.

Xander, on the other hand, was off the couch with a squeal, "I'll get it!"

I followed with a groan. I may have only been about three months pregnant, but I felt further along than that, my body creaked and didn't want to change positions once it got comfortable. Getting comfortable took forever. This was going to be a very long pregnancy.

I wasn't going to be able to catch Xander or lift him out of harm's way if he insisted on answering the front door at any time of day. I really needed to get a silent doorbell and a ring cam. Maybe I could keep him in check if he didn't know someone was at the door.

"Xander what did I say about opening the front door? We don't know…"

Xander squealed even more and giggled. I froze.

"Hey buddy! I missed you."

Alex stood there, looking handsome and like so much heartbreak. He lifted Xander into his arms.

"Where have you been? Mama said you had bizniss."

"I did. And I'm sorry it kept me away for so long." He looked up at me and our eyes locked. "I wasn't thinking straight."

The sincerity in his voice fluttered in my chest, like a butterfly, like hope.

"You might as well come in since you're here," I said.

Alex swung Xander down. "I can't believe how big you've gotten. It hasn't been that long, has it?" Xander scampered off, back to his movie, that we hadn't paused.

I know he was speaking to Xander, but Alex's eyes landed on my midsection. His eyes went wide, and his nostrils flared. He stood, his face stoic. It looked like he figured out I was pregnant.

That hope in my chest shriveled, would Alex realize he was the father? Or did he think so poorly of me? I was a single mother, I got a lot of judgement over my character because of that. Far too many people assumed I wasn't married, assumed that I made irresponsible choices, put the blame on me and never once asked about Xander's father. Not that any of it was their business. It wasn't.

Only now, I didn't want that from Alex. I already was on the receiving end of a lot of negative feelings from him, this was one more I didn't want. Not from him, especially not from him.

"Can we talk? It looks like we really need to." He stayed close to the door, even though I had invited him in.

209

"Xander and I were just finishing up a movie before bed. Would you like to join us? We can talk after he goes to bed." I tried not to let any emotion seep through to my voice. I didn't want Xander to know I was angry and nervous and a little but scared all at once. And I didn't want Alex to hear the desperation I felt.

Xander came back and tugged on Alex to go sit with him. Alex complied and walked over to the couch and sat.

Too many emotions crashed in my chest all at once. I didn't know what to think as we all sat together, like we had on so many nights before. Xander was mostly on Alex, but he didn't seem to mind.

And when the movie ended, Alex didn't say anything, he just picked up the limp, sleepy Xander and carried him upstairs to bed like so many times before. I had missed him being here, being a father. Being strong and lifting Xander like he weighed nothing. Helping to raise and care for our son, even though he didn't know their relationship. They had an emotional connection and the past few months had been hard on us both.

Xander hadn't understood why Alex no longer came over to have dinner and watch movies. He didn't understand why we couldn't go to the lake. I did my best to make sure he knew it wasn't his fault. It wasn't anyone's fault, but Alex had to work and run his business, and that was more important to him at that time. I did my best to keep my sadness and anger out of it for Xander. Mama and Daddy were getting a divorce, only I couldn't exactly tell him that because he didn't know Alex was his father, or that we were married.

Xander was happy to see Alex again. I would let them do the bedtime routine together. After all, this might be the last time. I swallowed back tears. I really did not want this to be the last time. I dared not hope that Alex showing up meant what I wanted so desperately for it to mean.

I stayed on the couch while Alex was upstairs tucking Xander into bed and reading him a short story. Even if Xander was asleep, Alex would sit and read to him. I think Alex liked reading to Xander. So, I waited while they finished the bed routine.

Alex came downstairs and hovered on the last step, looking at me.

I stared back. I really looked at him. He was rough around the edges. The sexy scruff was abandoned to messy scruff. His hair hadn't been brushed or styled in days. His clothes looked slept in. And his eyes looked as tired and sad as I felt.

"What are you doing here, Alex?" I finally managed to ask. "What is it you want from me?"

He pulled a folded up manilla envelope from his back pocket. He dropped it on the coffee table in front of me.

"Not this." He jabbed a finger in the direction of the crumpled envelope.

I didn't recognize it until I picked it up. The divorce papers. "I sent these in," I said, confused.

"You sent them back to the lawyer. They gave them to me so I could, I don't know, do some kind of a victory lap as I submitted them to the records office." He was quiet for a long time, pacing back and forth in the small living room.

"I couldn't do it." He stopped walking and stared at me. "I didn't understand why it had taken you so long to sign and send those papers back in, and then I had them in my hands. And I couldn't do it."

The breath stalled in my throat, and my heart clenched. That butterfly of hope in my chest spread its wings. I wanted to laugh, but I was terrified I was reading this all wrong.

"What is it that you want, Alex?"

I stood up, the crumpled divorce papers still in my hands.

He left me standing there and went into the kitchen. He rifled through drawer after drawer.

"What are you looking for?"

"This!" He brandished a long lighter I kept for candles.

He stretched out his hand to me and pulled me outside onto the back patio. Taking the envelope from my hands, he clicked the lighter until a flame appeared at the tip. He touched it to the corner of the envelope and held it there until it caught fire.

Flames licked around the papers and rapidly turned our divorce into char. Alex dropped everything onto the ground.

I stared at the flames, and then at him. He stepped close to me and touched my cheek. "I want to be married to you. I wanted that divorce so I could have you. But I didn't realize that we were already married. I wanted the family I didn't know I already had."

Tears fell from my eyes, and he brushed them aside with his thumb.

"I think I understand why you didn't tell me. How could you? I never gave you the chance."

I didn't know what to say, I struggled through emotions to be able to breathe. "Alex."

"Why didn't you tell me about Xander? Was it because I'm such an idiot that I couldn't recognize myself when he was staring right at me? I sent a picture of him to my mom, and she thought it was me. My head has been so far up my own ass, Sammy, that I couldn't see the truth when it was right in front of me."

"I..." I gulped in air. I needed to do this now before it got away, and I lost the chance, lost the moment. "I love you, Alex."

He wrapped himself around me and crushed me to his chest. His hands stroked my hair and back as he kissed my hair. "I never thought I'd hear those words from you. I thought I ruined it all."

He held me away, far enough so he could look me in my eyes. "I love you so much."

His lips crushed against mine. It was the kind of kiss that tried to make up for lost time in its ferocity. It wasn't gentle, it was intense. And then he changed tactics and the kiss softened. I was able to kiss him back. And I wanted to.

"Abigail Samantha Cole, please don't divorce me."

"You got my name right!" Tears still fell from my eyes, but I was laughing. "I'd like that very much. What do we do about that?" I pointed to the charred mess in my yard that had burnt divorce papers.

Alex shrugged. "I'll have my assistant tell the lawyers there was a change of plan."

"There have been many changes, haven't there?"

# 34

## ALEX

I pulled Sammy into me even closer. "I don't know about changes, how about I'm not getting in my own way anymore."

"I'll take that," she sniffed.

Happy tears I could handle from her, but not the sad ones.

"You're not mad about Xander?" she asked in a small tentative voice.

"Why would I be mad? He is a fabulous kid. Okay, maybe a little saddened. But I know better than to be mad, at least now I do. I think I understand why you did what you did. After all, there wasn't supposed to be anything between us. All this time I ignored the mistake I made on our wedding night."

"Mistake? Don't say that, Alex. It wasn't a mistake to me."

"It was outside our agreement, but you were so damned attractive."

Sammy giggled. "That's exactly what I thought. Maybe sleeping with you hadn't been the smartest move, but when was I going to get a guy with six pack abs again? I think I fell in love with you that night, Alex.

You made me feel special. You didn't have to, but you made me feel like a bride. And as a parting gift, I got Xander."

"He doesn't know who his father is, does he? You haven't told him."

"No, I haven't told him. Your name is not on the birth certificate. Alex, I walked away from that night in Vegas with a hefty check in my pocket that let me buy this place, and afford to go to school, with the understanding I was never to contact you, except through some lawyer's phone number your assistant had given me. I was well aware that I was not to ask for more money, and this was all a one-time deal."

I nodded. The prenuptial agreement had been very clear in its language. An initial sum to exchange hands, and that's it. Avoid each other if possible. Don't tell people who we were married to. It was a stupid man's idea for all the wrong reasons.

I was using something that should have been emotionally charged and special as a leverage for bad business. It had been egotistical of me, but it got me here.

"You know I picked computer programming because of you," she said.

I released her enough to look down at her. "You did what? Why would you do that?"

She tugged on my hand and led us back inside. "Come on, I'll tell you. You want a drink?"

"I'll have whatever you're having." I thought she would be drinking wine. She typically had a glass after Xander went to bed on the nights I was over.

"It's sweet tea. I hope that's okay." She handed me a tall glass of iced tea. I stared at it. When had she gotten glasses? She always had plastic. I suddenly missed her plastic cups. I remembered the first time I had asked about them.

"Why do you only have plastic cups in here?" I had been looking for a glass in her cupboards. None of the cups matched, and they certainly hadn't coordinated with her plates. It stood out in my memory because I had never been aware of the design of people's dishes before. They were there, in the background, not taking my attention away from the food or the company. And here Sammy's cupboard was a mismatched conglomeration of drink ware that dared to not match.

"Plastic doesn't break, it only spills. Five-year-old's drop cups and spill a lot."

"But Xander doesn't use these cups, he has lidded cups." I was so confused.

"I didn't say whose drinks he dropped and spilled. The kid has a talent to spill things that you'd think he couldn't reach. If plastic cups bother you that much, I'll go buy a set of glassware just for you."

At the time I wasn't certain if she had been teasing me over the glasses or not. As I stared at the glass of tea, I had to accept she hadn't been teasing.

"You got glasses," I mentioned.

"I did. It seemed a waste of time to try to return them, so I kept them. Iced tea really does taste better in glass."

"You got these for me?"

She nodded. "I've done a lot of things because of you, Alex."

"Yeah, what was that you were saying about programming?"

She chuckled and sat on the couch. I sat next to her. She snuggled in against me. I felt tension in my shoulders relax for the first time in weeks. Having Sammy back in my life, against my body, was the balm I didn't know that I needed.

"When I met you, I had just gotten out of a long-term relationship. David said he would support me while I went to college. He had just finished his degree in Hospitality Management. You know, running hotels. I was going to get the same degree, and we were going to run resorts and hotels all around the world together. But he changed his mind, and I was left on my own. College was still my plan, I didn't know how it was going to happen, but then I met you. I can't honestly say the initial thought was because of you or David. I just knew I wasn't going to go into hotel management, so instead I went into computer science, with a programming focus. At some point I hoped you would see and recognize the work I was doing."

I started laughing. She had gotten her wish. The work at Eyes On Care had definitely caught my attention. Okay so they had to come in and make a presentation for that to happen, but it happened.

"And I was too stupid to realize it was you." I spoke. "You know, you can stop me from calling myself stupid at any time here."

"I know. I think it just needs to sink in a bit more." She took a sip of her drink and batted her lashes at me.

"You are such a flirt," I said.

"No, I'm not. I worked really hard to resist you." Her lips puckered up in a pout with the slighted frown. She was adorably sexy.

I set my tea down, and carefully took hers from her hands, placing it on the table next to mine. I bundled her into my arms and lay back on the couch. Pulling her with me. Her weight on my legs was a pleasure I had denied myself.

"What are you doing?" She smiled down at me.

"Making it hard to resist me. Kiss me," I demanded.

Lucky for me, Sammy was in a compliant mood. Her lips were soft, and her body warm. She was right, I was stupid and that needed to sink in. I had let this woman go because my ego was hurt. Nothing more than some hurt feelings, and I almost destroyed something beautiful, something good.

I hummed into the soft kisses, hungry for more, but pleased with what I was getting. Sammy wiggled about. If she didn't calm down, there was definitely more going to happen. I wanted to take tonight slowly, savoring every second of being in her company, near her, with her.

"Are you staying?" She asked.

"If you allow me to. Yes, please."

"Are you going to move in here with me and Xander?"

I hadn't expected that question. I didn't know where we should live. We were married, and we were going to be together, it only made sense to live together.

"I hadn't thought about it. I guess we need a family home, don't we? My place downtown—"

"Isn't suitable for kids. It's lovely and posh, it really is, but it's not kid friendly," she said.

Sammy braced her arms across my chest and looked down at me like some kind of sphinx or large cat perched on my chest.

"The lake house?" I suggested.

"Too far from work. And I don't want to have to constantly worry about being on the water with small children. It's good for weekends, but not every day."

"Agreed. I guess I'll move in here while we look for a new home big enough for all of us."

"Really?" She looked at me with a bit of surprise. "I guess I thought you'd want to stay at your place until we found something we could agree on."

I reached up and brushed her hair back from where it fell in her face.

"I'm not leaving you again. I learn from my mistakes. Walking away from you was the biggest one I've ever made, and I'm not doing it again. I should have paid attention to you when we first got married. Checked in on you from time to time. Let my mother meet you. All of that. Maybe if I had taken being a husband, even if only on paper, a little more seriously, I could have avoided hurting you. I never want to do that again."

"Oh God, I'm going to have to meet your mother officially, aren't I?"

I laughed. "And we get to tell Xander I'm his father."

"That will be easy, he already loves you. Your mother, that's completely different. She thinks I'm some kind of two-bit floozy that lets you show her off while you have a wife you're ignoring."

I groaned. "You heard all of that?"

She nodded. "Heard some, read expressions mostly. Your uncle is a creep, and I did not appreciate him perving on me like that. Like he was going to wait for his turn." She shuddered above me.

I tightened my hands into fists. A low growl escaped my throat.

Sammy leaned down and kissed me. "I'll be fine, knowing you will be ready to defend my honor if he steps out of line. He'll be a lot easier to avoid than your mother."

"They seem to be a matched set," I told her.

Sammy shook her head. "I bet you tell your mother there are grand-children at stake, and she'll change her tune."

"She is going to spoil Xander rotten. Wait, did you say children, as in plural?" My heart skipped a beat.

# 35

## SAMMY

lex looked at me. His eyes went round, so did his mouth, and then the O spread into a smile. "You're kidding me?"

He sat up, forcing me onto my knees. I shifted and let gravity pull me back onto the couch. I ran a hand over my round belly. "How did you miss this? I'm already huge."

"You really aren't. Maybe there is a little baby bump going on." His eyes followed my hand, and then he reached out.

As he hesitated, I grabbed his wrist and placed his hand on my belly. He looked so excited, he didn't know what to say or do first.

"We're really having another baby?"

"We are, and you get to be around for this one."

Alex's face turned serious. "I never should have put you in a position like that. You will never have to face anything alone again."

"I like that. I like you." I sighed. "I love you."

Alex leaned over and kissed my middle before looking back up at me. His expression turned dark, and serious. "Say it again."

"What? I love you?"

"He growled low in his throat. 'That.' His hand scooped around the back of my neck. He drew me in close and then kissed me.

White hot lust shot through my body down to my toes. This was the kind of kiss I had missed from this man. When he kissed, he communicated. His needs, his caring, his apologies, everything could be conveyed in the way he kissed me. The message in this kiss was very clear. He wanted me.

It was a good thing, because I wanted him also.

I missed him desperately, and to have him back was a miracle. I wasn't going to waste time playing games. We would take it slow, if that's what either of us wanted. But we didn't. Desire burned hot and thinking was over.

Alex pulled at the buttons of his shirt until it was open. He spread my hand across his abs and over his pecs.

"So, you like my abs?"

"I like all of you," I confessed. "Your abs are like bonus points, or something."

"I like your abs," he said it in such a way I couldn't hear the joke.

"I don't have abs," I corrected.

"You do, yours are soft and rounded, and make babies." It was the sexiest thing I had ever heard.

He ran may hand down under his waist band. I gripped the fastening to his pants and his belt buckle.

"We need to take this behind a locked door," I managed. I was more than ready to help him strip down and let him take me on the couch. Fortunately, part of my brain registered that Xander could come exploring if he heard noises.

"Go upstairs, Sammy. I'll lock up."

I gulped; it was difficult with a dry mouth. Alex in competent husband mode was the sexiest he could possibly be. I had no idea that knowing he was my husband, the father of my children, that he was locking up the house for bed would be such an aphrodisiac, but it was.

He was more attractive in this moment than any other time I could remember. And for someone who was as insanely hot as he was, that meant a lot.

I didn't hurry up the stairs, I wanted to watch him. Watch my husband take care of us, watch him stalk toward me with every sexual intention announced in the way he moved.

"Up with you," he said when he caught me looking.

I headed upstairs. I looked in on Xander, he was asleep. I cycled the laundry and started the drier.

"Laundry? Now?" Alex asked as he reached the landing.

"I thought the drier noise might mask our noise."

He reached his hand out for mine. I took it and let him pull me into my bedroom. Our bedroom.

Alex took his shirt off completely, bunching it into a ball before tossing it aside. With a flick of his wrist, his belt buckle was undone, and the tops of his pants opened up.

I crawled onto the bed and pulled my tunic over my head.

"Allow me, you're like a gift I long to unwrap." He took the shirt from my hands and ran his hand up my back as he placed small kisses along my shoulder and across the tops of my breasts.

I shuddered with anticipation and excitement. The small hair at the base of my neck stood on end.

"Are you cold?"

"No," my voice quavered. "I like it, keep going."

His fingers tailed across my skin, leaving trails of heated skin. His mouth, his lips, teeth, tongue, nibbled, licked, and bit. He removed my bra. My nipples were already tight with excitement.

I sighed as he cupped one breast into a large warm hand. And that sigh turned into a gasp as he pulled my other nipple into his mouth. He tugged at it before running his tongue over me, and then sucking it into his mouth again.

I squirmed against his touch. He needed more hands. I needed to know what to do with mine. I wanted to touch all of his skin, thread my fingers through his hair and hold him to me. There were too many options, too many decisions, and I could not think straight. His mouth was on me and that's all I ever wanted. All I ever needed.

He pushed up onto his knees. Our eyes locked. It was as if we both knew it was time. I pressed my heels into the mattress as he tugged my leggings off. He got off the bed, divested himself of the rest of his clothes and then returned to me. He covered us in a sweeping motion that made me think of a vampire with his cape, covering his victim from sight.

I ran my legs over his, touched his skin, caressed the plains of him. I stroked up his leg until I found his cock. He was thick and hot. His balls were soft under my touch. He moaned and hissed as I explored his body as if it were for the first time. In a way it almost was. Outside our wedding night, this was the first time we were together as a married couple, with both of us knowing. I know for me, it was different.

"How do we do this?" Alex asked.

"It hasn't been that long since we stopped talking that you forgot how to make love to me?" I teased.

"I meant with the baby. How do I make love to my pregnant wife and not hurt you, or the baby?"

"I would guess we just go slow. If something doesn't feel right, we stop, shift."

Alex rolled into me, kneeing my legs apart. He lifted my legs over his hips. His cock caressed my folds and bumped against my clit.

"You tell me if I'm too heavy." Concern filled his expression; his brow was pulled together and he looked stern with concentration.

"Relax. I'll be fine, if you manage to get on with it." I laughed. This was wonderful, his concern, actually communicating and asking my needs. If I wasn't already in love with him, I would be because of right now.

He slid into me. My eyes fluttered closed. It was so perfect to have him in me this way. I rolled my hips. His hands held tight to my thighs as he lifted me enough to not make the position awkward. He slid back and flexed his thighs, drove forward, filling me completely.

My entire body felt alight with energy. I was all nerves with twitches and shivers. It felt as if the second he touched me, I started to orgasm, and it kept rolling over me pulsing and leaving me weak. It was the most amazing sensation. I didn't want it to end, and yet I felt as if I was driving toward some glorious purpose.

I rolled my hips when I could remember to move, but mostly I tried not to let out loud moaning cries and held on to whatever I could get a grip of. Alex's arm, his shoulder, the bedding.

He pressed into me, pushing me closer and closer. But how could I get someplace I already was? My inner walls already pounded and throbbed, holding him, pulling on him.

And then I was a starburst. I was light and an ever-expanding particle. I wanted to call out Alex's name, I wanted to cry for joy, but all sound was trapped in my throat as I forgot how to breathe, how to be human while my body was fireworks and magic.

Alex followed me into the night with a growl. He pressed hard against me, as he filled me with his release. When he could move again, he was very careful of me. He rolled to the side and pulled me into his arms.

"Are you okay? I didn't crush you?" The overly concerned expression was back.

I cupped his cheek. "Oh, you crushed me good. Everything is alright. I love you, that was amazing."

Alex's heavy breathing turned into a chuckle. "It was. I think I'd be required to ask you to marry me if we weren't all ready after that. You will stay with me, Sammy, say we'll stay married."

"We're already married, aren't we?" It was kind of unreal, and hard to wrap my head around it.

"Yeah, we are. We're a family, officially, if you want."

"Alex, I couldn't be happier to remain married to you. After all this time, we get to be together. It's amazing. You're amazing."

He kissed me. "We're amazing."

"We are. How do we tell people we're married? Should I change my name now?"

"I think Sammy Stone has a very good ring to it. We need to go ring shopping. My wife isn't walking around without a ring on her finger. Let them think it was a quickie Vegas marriage. They won't be wrong, only off by a few years."

I was married to a very smart man.

## 36

# EPILOGUE

## ALEX

*A year later*

The buyout of Eyes On Care went through as it originally had been planned before the upset of learning Sammy's true identity. Foundation Network Communications absorbed the business, and the employees into our existing structure, keeping as many processes in place as we could. Within six months Eyes On Care changed its name to Eyes On, and began expanding into elder care while simultaneously reaching into other regions.

There was no swooping in like vultures to pick at the remains of a destroyed business. The business hadn't been destroyed; Sammy's finances had been sound. Sloppy from what she told me, but sound. Unfortunately, this upset a few people on my end of things. They needed to realize that just because this was business, it didn't mean I needed to continue to hurt Sammy. Business didn't need to be cutthroat. Agreements could be reached that benefited everyone, and in this case, it did.

She was my wife, the mother of my children. I loved her and it was my job to protect her, personally and in business. Vanessa left, and for their own reasons, Harper and Mandy followed. For a while I had thought I lost competent assistants, but I gained everything and more with Sammy.

"No, I'm positive." She spoke as if she were having a conversation, but the only person near her was the baby, Lexi, as they sat on the lounge. A tell-tale, white earbud gave away that Sammy was on the phone. She swung her legs over the side of the lounge and stood, hefting the baby onto her hip.

I sat on the edge of the sandbox where mom and Xander scooped sand into toy dump trucks and moved it around. She joined us for a weekend at the lake. It was becoming a habit of hers. Now that she had grandchildren, she seemed like a different woman. She never would have played in a sandbox with me as a child. Uncle Roy no longer followed in her wake or dragged her along in his.

Whatever there had been between them, it was over now. He continued to butt into the day-to-day of business at Foundation Network Communications, but he no longer used my mom as some form of emotional manipulation.

Sammy walked back and forth across the yard in a serious discussion with someone. "I can do that where I am. Look, I appreciate your offer. I really do, but I just don't think you can offer a package that's going to lure me away from where I am now. You, too. Goodbye."

She crossed to where we all were and sat in a deck chair, staying out of the sand.

"Who was that?" I asked.

"It's the recruiter for that start-up in San Jose. They think now that I've successfully started, sold off, and grown Eyes On Care that I'm ready to do that all over again."

"You know, Sammy, you shouldn't be working. You have babies," Mother said.

"I know I don't have to, but I like working. I barely work as it is. I consult. And that's plenty," Sammy replied.

"Pish, Alex, why is your wife working at all? You make more than enough money for her to pursue other interests."

"I like to work Mother Stone. I've been working most of my life. I don't have other interests," Sammy sighed.

"You have your children. They should be your focus," Mother said.

"They are my focus. The kids are my hobbies. Or maybe the kids are the work, and the job is the hobby to give me a break from them."

"You should join one of my committees. Fundraising is a worthy pursuit."

"Mom, she said she likes to work. Not everyone is interested in putting on big elaborate parties and brushing shoulders with the financial elite."

She huffed at me. "You only get away with saying that because you are the financial elite. And it's not about brushing shoulders. It's the spectacle, the fashion, it's fun. I've thrown hundreds of parties, raised hundreds of thousands of dollars. It's worthwhile, it's fulfilling. I think that if I ever had to have a job, mind you, I don't think about this frequently, but I think I would have been a spectacular wedding planner. You know I never was allowed to throw you a proper wedding reception. It would have been glorious. Or would your mother have taken charge?"

Sammy smiled calmly. "My mother would not have taken charge of the wedding planning. She wouldn't have been there, even if she had known about it. Change of subject please."

"I was just asking—"

"Mother," I tried not to snap. Xander didn't need the adults talking over his head bickering. I shook my head at her.

"Fine. But I want to plan a party for you. We had so much fun at Xander's sixth birthday, didn't we?"

"That was the best. Can we do pony rides again?" Xander jumped into the conversation once he heard his name.

"It was, wasn't it. We could do that again this year, but we could also do something different, like get circus clowns, and have acrobats." Mother's eyes showed, she was in her element, planning something over the top.

She had been insistent on hosting Xander's birthday pretty much the second she met him. He was the perfect grandchild, and as predicted, spoiled rotten. If she wanted to bring in an entire circus performance to set up on the front lawn of her mansion, she was welcome to it.

I was a little surprised she hadn't started planning Lexi's first birthday yet. At just shy of six months, she was the most perfect, delightful baby. I wouldn't trade one sleepless night helping to care for her for anything in the world.

If Xander looked like me as a baby, then Lexi had to look like Sammy. Sammy didn't have baby pictures; she didn't have the kind of family that would have treasured those moments properly. Together we made sure that our children were loved and adored. And through Lexi, we could see what Sammy would have looked like as a baby. Beautiful. My wife was simply beautiful.

Mother was still talking about parties. I tuned back in, and wished I hadn't. This was going to turn into an argument if she didn't drop the topic.

"I have been blessed with such adorable grandchildren. I'm still going to be sad thinking about having missed your wedding. You know, your tenth anniversary is only a few years away. It's not too soon to think about booking a location. You could renew your vows. Get back into pre-baby shape."

"Change of subject please," Sammy said through clenched teeth.

"Oh, don't mind me. I've never planned a wedding. It's fun to think about."

"Then think about it for anyone else but me and Alex. We are already happily married."

"Of course, you are, dear. I didn't mean that you weren't. You simply started out so unconventionally. Your family and friends didn't get the opportunity to celebrate with you."

Sammy sighed and stood up. "The friends I have now are not the same people I was friends with when Alex and I got married. They wouldn't have been there anyway."

"That's exactly what I'm saying."

Lexi squirmed and leaned as if she wanted out of Sammy's hold. "Why don't you play with Nana."

Sammy handed Lexi over to Mother, instantly changing her focus from the topic of wedding party planning to the baby in her arms.

"Are you going to help us?" Mother placed Lexi in front of her and the baby grabbed handfuls of sand.

Sammy whirled on me and gave me a hard stare.

"Excuse us, will you?" I was out of my chair and followed Sammy into the house. "What is it? What did she say this time?"

"What did she say? Weren't you listening? She thinks she's planning a big wedding for us in less than three years."

"I can't believe we'll have been married for ten years so soon." I smiled and pulled her into my arms.

Sammy thumped me on the chest. "Alex, that's not the point and you know it. I don't want to re-enact some wedding ceremony just to keep your mother happy. I've had my wedding; it was perfectly acceptable. Better even, because the only people there were the one who mattered."

I agreed, it had been just us and legal witnesses. "Though I do like the idea of dressing up and showing you off."

"I'm okay with that, but not the wedding part. We can have a party if she wants, but I'm not wearing a wedding dress. You know what would be better?"

I shrugged. "What would make you the happiest?"

"For our tenth anniversary, whisk us away, all four of us, take us someplace magical, and don't invite your mother."

I kissed my wife on her nose. "I know just the place. You and the kids will love it. Mother will hate it and not invite herself."

"Thank you. I love you."

I took advantage of being alone for a moment and kissed her, kissed her properly letting her know that I loved her more than anything.

.

# 37

# EXCERPT: TWINS FOR THE PLAYBOY

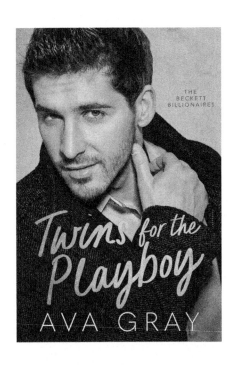

**player and a princess could never be together.**

**They shouldn't even *pretend* to be in love...**

I wish someone had told me this before I said yes.

Agreeing to play the role of a girlfriend for Crew Beckett's billionaire family was a gamble.

I looked like a silly girl when I couldn't stop admiring him in his suit.

His messy brown hair continued to remind me of the night we spent together.

He didn't know that my family was royalty.

Scratch that, he *still* doesn't know that secret of mine.

But just as he needed to clean up his reputation with a fake girlfriend...

I also needed a man to keep my family from forcing me to return to Ambrosia.

Taking on my royal responsibilities terrifies me.

Being in the arms of this player makes me feel the kind of princess I want to be.

Telling him what's in my heart is risky.

But I have to reveal the other secret I'm keeping from him.

**Everything could crumble down once he finds out that I'm not only pregnant with his twins... *but I'm also not who he thinks I am.***

## Noelle

Stifling a sigh, I tell myself the date isn't going as badly as it feels. That I'm just being dramatic and the worry gnawing at my gut is due to the ticking clock that my parents have set for me.

But the truth is, the man sitting across the table from me is not my type of person.

As much as I would like him to be, he just isn't the one.

My attention wanders over the other diners in the restaurant, specifically to the attractive couple at the table next to us. They look to be in their late 20s and they can't keep their eyes or hands off each other. I watch him lean close and whisper something in her ear. The woman's face flushes, and she lets out a low, seductive laugh full of promise.

Longing and a sliver of jealousy spears through me.

I've never experienced that kind of connection with anyone. No man has ever gazed deeply into my eyes and whispered naughty secrets in my ear. It's something I yearn for but, for whatever reason, it never seems to happen.

I've been under a lot of pressure to find someone and settle down these last few years and I turned to online dating when it didn't happen organically. So much for that, I think, and look back over at my date who is currently sporting breadcrumbs in his beard. He's also been talking about himself nonstop since we sat down and hasn't bothered to ask me a single question.

The last thing I need in my life is a narcissistic asshole.

Strike that. Another narcissistic asshole because how could I forget Alec Graham?

"Excuse me," I say, the moment he pauses between breaths. Before he can continue talking about himself, I quickly stand up. "I'm going to use the restroom. Be right back."

I hurriedly turn and head for the bathroom in the corner. Once I sneak inside, I pull my phone out of my purse and text my best friend, Katie Halloran.

*S.O.S.*, I type and hit send.

That's all I need to write. It's our code when we need immediate saving from a date gone bad. Typical protocol means she will call me in exactly three to five minutes with some kind of "emergency" that will require me to leave right away.

I fluff my medium-length blonde hair, fix the eyeliner under my blue eyes and pull in a deep breath. Unfortunately, the uber perfect guy who I've been messaging all week is nothing like I had hoped he would be.

Another disappointing date for the books.

There are millions of people living in New York City? Why is it so hard to find a decent guy?

*Maybe it's me,* I think, and push the bathroom door open. Are my expectations too high? All I want is a man who is kind, respectful and who listens to me when I speak. I mean, really listens. Not someone who just drones on and on about himself for 45 minutes straight while he guzzles down three beers and devours an entire steak.

Oh, and I can't forget the bread. He ate the whole basket without offering me one slice.

Am I asking too much?

I don't think so.

As I sit back down at the table, Andy immediately starts talking about a new client he signed and bragging about how the account is worth almost $100 million dollars. I'm still not exactly sure what he does—something about managing or investing rich people's money. Stock market stuff which I find incredibly boring, but I was willing to listen and learn more. Too bad he didn't reciprocate the courtesy.

When my phone rings, it's like a lifeline is thrown to me. I glance down at the caller ID and see Katie's name. "Oh, I should probably take this. It could be important. I'm sorry," I tell him and answer the call. "Hello?"

"Hey, babe. I got your S.O.S. Damn, it's going that bad? It hasn't even been an hour yet."

"Oh, hi. What? Are you serious?" I put just the right amount of surprise and concern in my voice then look up at Andy with wide eyes, hoping my acting skills are convincing. Oh, hell, at this point, what do I care? I just want to get the hell out of here.

"I had high hopes for this one," Katie says, voice full of disappointment.

"Flooding? Oh no! I'll be right there." I hang up and look across the table where Andy is finally listening. Too late. I stand up, tossing some money on the table and swinging my purse over my shoulder. "My apartment flooded. Pipe burst." I give him a small shrug and push my chair back in.

"Oh, well, that sucks."

"Gotta go. Sorry." I turn and practically jog over to the exit and out the door. The June evening is warm, but luckily, it's not humid. I lift my hand, flag down a taxi and hop inside. After telling him my address, I sit back and watch the city lights go by. I don't have a driver's license because, well, I've never needed one. Growing up back home, I always had a private chauffeur and living now in Manhattan, even though there's a plethora of choices from Ubers to taxis to the subway, my parents insisted that I have a driver always available. His name is Fred Wright and I adore him.

Since it's Fred's wife's birthday today, I gave him the day off and told him to take her out. But I don't mind and enjoy taking public transportation.

A part of me wishes I did have a license because I would love to drive a car. Roll the windows down, push the pedal against the floor and let the wind blow my hair all over the place as I cruise down a back road somewhere in the middle of nowhere.

Complete freedom.

It's something I crave and yearn for with every fiber of my being. It's also the one luxury I will never be allowed as long as my parents have their say. Although I'm nearly 28, my life isn't fully my own. I was born into a family with duties, traditions and endless responsibilities. And although I've managed to escape them for the last five years, the noose around my neck is beginning to tighten again. The panic is tangible, and my time is running out fast.

My 28th birthday is in exactly four weeks. If I don't find a man by then, someone I could potentially fall in love with and marry, then I have to return home to my country and the overwhelming duties waiting for me to assume. The thought makes my stomach churn.

Because let's face it—I'm not going to meet anyone that fast who I could present to my parents as my fiancé. It's completely unrealistic. I've been searching since the moment I arrived in NYC five years earlier. With four weeks left, it would take a major miracle for me to find love.

Returning to Ambrosia, the small Mediterranean island where I grew up, is the last thing I want to do. It feels like I just escaped. I'm lucky my parents allowed me to come here and go to school. I studied art history and loved every moment of it. But now the idea of leaving Manhattan, the friends I've made, the life I was hoping to have here…

It's killing me.

When the taxi pulls up outside my building, I get out and pull my keycard out of my purse. It's a pretty fancy place and even though I told my parents I didn't need to live in such an extravagant building, they insisted. The door opens after I swipe it and I walk over to my private elevator which zips me straight up to the top floor.

Fifty-two floors later, I step right into my foyer and drop my purse on the bench. Katie pokes her head out of the kitchen and holds up a pint of my favorite Ben and Jerry's ice cream.

"I come bearing gifts," she says with a lopsided smile.

"Thanks. I need it." I head across the plush carpet and walk into the very large, modern kitchen. Katie offers me a spoon and the container of Cherry Garcia. I shove the spoon into the frozen deliciousness and scoop out a big scoop. "Mmm," I moan as the comforting flavor fills my mouth.

"So, what happened?" Katie asks and plops down on a stool at the granite-topped island.

"Oh, just the usual," I say and sit down beside her. "The perfectly normal, nice guy I was talking to all week turned out to be a narcissist who could only talk about himself and what an asset he is to his company." I roll my eyes and take another big bite of ice cream. "He didn't ask me one question. Just rambled on and one about his work and life."

"Well, that sucks."

"Oh, and he ate all the bread they brought us when we first sat down. Then I had to stare at the crumbs caught in his beard. I tried to ignore them, but I couldn't."

We both burst out laughing.

"The dating scene is absolutely brutal," Katie acknowledged. "Like one good guy for every 200 duds."

"You're lucky you found Matthew."

"You don't have to tell me twice," she says and eats some more of her peanut butter ice cream. "But here's the thing. It always happens when you least expect it."

"So they say," I murmur and stab my spoon against the frozen edge, digging for a cherry.

"It's true," she insists. "When I met Matthew, I had just broken up with Rick and sworn men off. Not to sound like a cliche, but when it's meant to be, it'll happen."

"That's all fine and dandy, but I'm running out of time. Fast," I remind her.

"I know, sweetie," she says sympathetically. "When's the last time you talked to your mom and dad?"

"I keep dodging their calls," I admit. "But I'm going to have to answer sooner than later. I can't believe how fast the last five years went by and now I'm going to have to go back to Ambrosia."

God, I want to cry.

"And be a princess again," she says softly.

I nod, feeling utterly miserable. "It's not even just about returning. There's also Alec."

"Who has arranged marriages nowadays?" Katie asks and frowns. "That's so archaic."

"Royalty," I inform her. "And it is archaic. And so damn depressing that I'm not sure what else I can do at this point. Except ball my eyes out and fly back home in four weeks. Forever."

Katie reaches over and lays a hand on my arm. "I know you've tried but tell them again how happy you are here and that you want to stay."

I shake my head. "I made a promise. If I didn't meet anyone special here in four years—which then turned into five—I would return home and carry out my royal responsibilities."

"I'm sorry, Noelle. I wish there was something I could do to help."

"My parents gave me a chance which is more than most would do in their position. Being their only child, it's up to me to assume the reins and leadership. I wasn't able to figure out my future so now they're going to do it for me."

"But you're not in love with Alec Graham!"

"Not even close," I concede, my voice dismal. "He's going to be thrilled. All he ever wanted was to be part of the royal family. Ugh."

"Don't give up hope yet," Katie says and gets up. She wanders over to the cupboard and pulls two wine glasses out. "Okay, enough sugar. Now we need alcohol."

I nod and accept the glass while she pulls out an expensive bottle of my favorite red wine made in Ambrosia. It's sweet and decadent. The perfect dessert wine. She pours me a very full glass.

"There has to be something we can do. I don't want my best friend to live on the other side of the world," Katie says.

"Other than falling in love and finding a man that I can present to my parents as my future husband and prince..." My voice trails off. "There's not anything else I can do. Nothing except pack my bags and return to Ambrosia."

Katie shakes her head. "I refuse to accept that answer. There has to be something we can do. Some way we can convince your parents to give you more time. One more year!"

"That was my argument last year and they barely agreed."

Unfortunately for me, there was only one way I'd be staying in New York City: I had to find my prince.

And in a city full of frogs, that was turning into a very hard and seemingly unrealistic goal.

**Read the complete story HERE!**

# SUBSCRIBE TO MY MAILING LIST

I hope you enjoyed reading this book.

In case you would like to receive information on my latest releases, price promotions, and any special giveaways, then I would recommend you to subscribe to my mailing list.

You can do so now by using the subscription link below.

**SUBSCRIBE TO AVA GRAY's MAILING LIST!**